"I'm going to give you twenty-four hours to think about my proposition. I'll leave the engagement ring here. Try not to misplace it."

"I may not agree to anything."

"Your call." Leo shrugged. "I anticipate six weeks of inconvenience. Think about the trade-off." He stood up and glanced at his watch to find that far more time had gone by than he'd expected. "Just one more thing to consider..."

Sam had scrambled to her feet, but she was still keeping her distance. She wasn't going to touch this offer with a barge pole. Was she? It smacked of blackmail, and surely any form of deceit, however well intended, was a bad thing...

"What's that?" She eyed him warily.

"You asked why you're perfect for this...arrangement." He kept his eyes fixed on her face as he began putting on his coat. "You understand the rules. I don't mean the rules that involve pretending...I mean the rules that dictate that this isn't for real. You're not a woman who might get it into her head that a fake engagement might turn into a real engagement."

"No. I'm not." Because there was no way he would ever consider getting engaged for real to someone like her. She'd never wanted to slap someone as much as she wanted to slap him.

"So we're on the same page," Leo drawled, tilting his head at her. "Always a good thing. I'll be in touch tomorrow evening for your decision...my wife-to-be."

Cathy Williams can remember reading Harlequin books as a teenager, and now that she is writing them, she remains an avid fan. For her, there is nothing like creating romantic stories and engaging plots, and each and every book is a new adventure. Cathy lives in London, and her three daughters—Charlotte, Olivia and Emma—have always been, and continue to be, the greatest inspirations in her life.

Books by Cathy Williams

Harlequin Presents

The Italian Titans

One Night With Consequences

Visit the Author Profile page at Harlequin.com for more titles.

Cathy Williams

BOUGHT TO WEAR
THE BILLIONAIRE'S RING

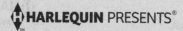

HARLEQUIN PRESENTS®

Recycling programs
for this product may
not exist in your area.

ISBN-13: 978-0-373-21313-9

Bought to Wear the Billionaire's Ring

First North American publication 2017

Copyright © 2017 by Cathy Williams

Printed in U.S.A.

BOUGHT TO WEAR
THE BILLIONAIRE'S RING

CHAPTER ONE

'So…' Leo Morgan-White handed his father a glass of claret and sat down opposite him.

Harold had travelled all the way from Devon and had been delivered only half an hour previously by his chauffeur. It had been a surprise visit, which he had been told by his agitated father the evening before couldn't wait.

Despite this, they had yet to get down to business and, although Leo knew what it concerned, he was still puzzled as to why it couldn't have waited until the weekend when he would gladly have travelled to Devon.

But his father was emotional and impulsive and so it was nigh on impossible to gauge just how important his news actually was. Leo couldn't think that it would be important enough to have him rushing up to London, a city he tried to avoid at all costs.

'Too noisy,' he was fond of complaining. 'Too crowded. Too polluted. Too many expensive shops selling nonsense. A man can't hear himself think there! You know what I say, Leo—if you can't hear the grass growing, you're in the wrong place!'

'What's going on?' Leo now asked, reclining back and stretching out his long legs. He carefully placed his glass on the table next to him and linked his fingers loosely on his stomach.

His father's eyes were glistening and he looked on the verge of bursting into tears. His chin was wobbling and his breathing was suspiciously uneven. Leo knew from experience that it was always better to ignore these signs of an imminent breakdown and focus on what needed to be discussed. His father needed very little encouragement when it came to shedding tears.

It was a trait Leo had thankfully not inherited. Indeed, anyone would have been forgiven for thinking that the two were not related at all as, both temperamentally and physically, they couldn't have been more different.

Where Leo was long, lean and darkly handsome, a legacy from his Spanish-born mother, his father was of an average height and rotund.

And where Leo was cool, composed and cutthroat, his father was unapologetically emotional and fond of dramatic outbursts. Leo's mother had died a little over a decade ago, when

Leo had been twenty-two, and he remembered her as a tall, ridiculously good-looking woman who, having inherited her family's business at the tender age of nineteen, had been very clever, very shrewd and who had a natural flair for running a company. On paper, she and his father should have had nothing in common and yet theirs had been a match made in heaven.

In an age where men went out to work and women kept the home fires burning, his home life had been the opposite. His mother had run the family business, which she had brought from Spain with her, while his father, a hugely successful author, had stayed at home and written.

In a weird and wonderful way, opposite poles had attracted.

Leo loved his father deeply and his eyes narrowed as Harold carefully took a sheet of paper from his pocket and pushed it across the table to his son.

He fluttered one hand and looked away, before saying in a shaky voice, '*That* woman has emailed me this...'

Leo eyed the sheet of paper but didn't reach for it. 'I've told you that you need to stop getting yourself worked up about this, Dad. I have my lawyers working on it. It's all going to be all right. You just have to be patient. The woman can fight all she likes but she won't be getting anywhere.'

'Just you read what she has to say, Leo. I... I can't bring myself to read it out loud.'

Leo sighed. 'How is the book coming along?'

'Don't try and distract me,' his father responded mournfully. 'I haven't been able to write a word. I've been too worried about this business to spare a thought for how DI Tracey is going to solve the case. In fact, I don't care! At this rate, I may never put pen to paper again. It's all very well for you business types...adding up numbers and sitting round conference tables...'

Leo stifled a smile. He was worth billions and did a lot more than just add up numbers and sit round conference tables.

'She's made threats,' Harold said, sucking in a shaky breath. 'You read the email, Leo. The woman says she's going to fight for custody and she's going to win. She says she's spoken to her lawyer and although Sean stated in his will that Adele was to come to you if anything happened to him, Louise never agreed and now they're both gone. All that matters is that Adele's well-being would be put in jeopardy if she stays with that woman.'

'Heard it all before.' Leo drained his claret and stood up, massaging the back of his neck as he strolled towards the expanse of glass that separated him from the busyness of London which never stopped, even in the most prestigious of postcodes.

His apartment occupied the top two floors of an impressive Georgian building. He had hired the most prestigious architect in the city who had cleverly used the vast space to create an elegant blend of old and new, leaving the coving and fireplaces and ceiling details intact while changing pretty much everything else. The result was an airy, four-bedroomed testament to what could be done when money was no object.

The walls were adorned with priceless modern art. The decor was muted—shades of grey and cream. People's mouths fell open the second they walked through the door but Leo was barely aware of his surroundings. They didn't intrude and that was the main thing.

'This is different, Leo.'

'Dad,' he said patiently, 'it's not. Gail Jamieson wants to hang on to her granddaughter for dear life because she thinks it's a conduit to my money but she's utterly ill-equipped to look after a five-year-old child. She'll be especially ill-equipped when my money stops and she has to fend for herself. The fact is…this is a case I will win. I don't want to throw money at the woman but if I have to, I will. She'll take it and head for the hills because, like her daughter before her, Gail is a money-grabbing gold-digger who's not above manipulating a situation for her own advantage. Need I remind you of the train of events that led Sean to Australia?'

His father grunted and Leo didn't push it. They both knew Sean for the man he had been.

Seven years younger than Leo, Sean had arrived on their doorstep at the age of sixteen, along with his mother, Georgia Ryder, with whom Leo's father had fallen head over heels in love less than a year after Leo's mother had died.

From the very beginning Sean, an incredibly pretty boy with overlong blond hair and light blue eyes, had been lazy and spoiled. Once his mother had a ring on her finger and free access to the Morgan-White millions, he had quickly become even more demanding and petulant. His studies had fallen by the wayside and, cosseted by his mother, he had spent his time hanging around with a gang of like-minded teenagers who had gravitated towards him like bees round a honeypot. It hadn't been long before drugs had crept into the scene.

Leo's father, with the ink on the marriage certificate barely dry, had woken up from his grief-induced daze and realised the size of the mistake he had made. He didn't want a blonde bombshell twenty years his junior pretending to love him when the only thing she loved was his money. He wanted to mourn the passing of the woman he had loved. He wanted uninterrupted misery.

Leo had taken Sean to one side and had given him the talking-to of his life, which had done no good at all. The opposite. Within two years Sean had dropped out of school. Within four, he had become heavily involved with Louise Jamieson, an enthusiastic member of the club for losers to which he belonged, and by the time his mother, after a series of unabashed flings with men her own age, had quit her marriage to Harold and begun her bid for as much alimony as she could get, Sean had moved to Australia with a heavily pregnant wife.

By this time Leo's father had all but given up. His writing had stopped completely and his editor's frantic communications had remained unanswered. He had become a virtual recluse and Leo had been left to pick up the pieces.

Unchecked, Georgia had spent vast sums of money on everything under the sun, from diamonds and tiaras to horses, cars and exotic holidays abroad, while she still had access to her soon-to-be ex-husband's bank accounts. She had lavished money on her son. Leo, building his own career, had not had his eye sufficiently on the ball to have stopped the momentum.

By the time the nuts and bolts of the messy divorce had been ironed out, his father had been left with a bank account that had been severely dented. The fact that he hadn't put pen to paper for years hadn't helped.

Then Georgia was catapulted to her death off a hairpin bend on a road while vacationing in Italy with the money she had squeezed out of Harold. Left to make the decision, Leo would have thrown Sean to the wolves but his father, much softer and with a conscience that could be pricked by almost anything, had continued to send money to his former stepson. He had dug deep to make sure Sean's daughter had all the things he would have given her, had she lived in the same country. He had begged for photos and had been thrilled with the handful of pictures Sean had emailed over.

He had tried to make plans to visit but Sean had always had an excuse.

Georgia had been a disaster and her son had been no less of a catastrophe and, unlike his sentimental father, Leo wasn't going to allow emotions to hold sway over the outcome of this bizarre custody battle.

He would win because he always won. Louise's mother, whom he had met once when he went to Australia, had confirmed all his suspicions that the last thing she was concerned about was the welfare of her grandchild. She was an appalling woman and no appalling woman was going to get the better of him.

'She says that it doesn't matter how much money you have to fight this, Leo. She's going to win because you're not fit to be a father to Adele.'

Leo stilled. His father's eyes had welled up. Reluctantly, he retrieved the paper from where his father had earlier shoved it to him and carefully read the email that had been sent by Ms Jamieson.

'Now you see what I mean, Leo.' His father's voice shook. 'And the woman has a point. You have to see that.'

'I see nothing of the sort.'

'You don't lead a responsible life.' Harold's voice firmed. 'Not as far as bringing up a young child is concerned. You spend half your life out of the country...'

'How else am I supposed to run my companies?' Leo interjected, enraged that a woman who appeared to have the morals of a sewer rat should dare to criticise him. 'From an armchair at home?'

'That's not the point. The point is that you *do* spend a great part of the year out of the country. How is that supposed to be good for the well-being of a five-year-old child? Furthermore, she's not wrong when she says that you...' His hands fluttered in a gesture of resignation and disappointment.

Leo's mouth thinned. He knew that the choices he made when it came to women did not fill his father's heart with glee. He knew that Harold would have done anything to have seen him happily settled down with a nice, respectable girl who would have those home fires burning for him when he returned home after a long day toiling in the fields.

It wasn't going to happen. Leo had too much first-hand experience of how life could be derailed when emotions got in the way of common sense and good judgement. No matter that his father had adored his wife—when Mariela Morgan-White had died, he had been left a broken man. Yes, some idiots might fall for that hoary old chestnut about it being better to have loved and lost than never to have loved at all, but Leo had never signed up to that.

His father might not have agreed with Leo's choices but he had stopped trying to take him to task about them, and this was the first time in years that he had voiced his disappointment.

'Your face is never out of the papers,' Harold admonished, dabbing his eyes and then looking sternly at his son. 'There's always some… some silly little thing hanging on to your arm, batting her eyelashes at you.'

Leo flushed with irritation. 'We've covered this ground already.'

'And we'll cover it again, son.' Harold sniffed and, just like that, Leo realised it was as though the energy and life force had been sucked out of him, leaving behind a shell. He was an aging man and it seemed as though he had suddenly lost the will to live.

'You choose to do what you like when it comes to…women,' his father said quietly. 'And I know better now than to try and point you in the right direction. But this is more than being *just about you*. The woman claims that you're morally unfit to take guardianship of the child.'

Leo pushed his hands through his hair and shook his head. 'I'll take care of it,' he said grimly.

Theoretically, he and his father could simply reach an agreement to pull the plug on the money. Sean, after all, hadn't been in any way related to either of them, but he knew and personally agreed that the child should not be allowed to suffer because of the mistakes of her parents. Like it or not, she was a moral responsibility.

'It's a worst-case scenario.' His father shook his head and pressed his fingers to his eyes.

'You're upsetting yourself, Dad.'

'Wouldn't you if you were in my shoes?' He looked up. 'Adele is important to me and I cannot lose.'

'If the law refuses to budge—' Leo spread his hands in a gesture of frustration '—then there's only so much I can do. I can't kidnap the child and then hide her until she turns eighteen.'

'No, but there *is* something you can do…'

'I'm struggling to think what.'

'You could get engaged. I'm not saying married, but engaged. You could present the court with the sort of responsible image that might persuade them into thinking that you're a good bet as a father figure for Adele.'

Leo stared at his father in silence. He wondered whether the events of the past few weeks had finally pushed the man over the edge. Either that or he had misheard every single word in that sweeping, unbelievable statement.

'I could get engaged...?' Leo shook his head with rampant incredulity. 'Do you suggest I purchase a suitable candidate online?'

'Don't be stupid, son!'

'Then I'm not following you.'

'If you need to present the image of a solid, dependable, *normal* human being with a *serious* and *suitable* woman by your side, then I don't know why you wouldn't do that. For me. For Adele.'

'Serious and suitable woman?' Leo spluttered. He didn't do either serious *or* suitable when it came to women. He did frivolous and highly unsuitable. He liked it that way. No involvement, easy to dispatch. If they enjoyed his money, then that was fine because he wasn't going to marry any of them. When it came to women, the revolving door that brought them in and took them out was efficient and worked for him.

'Samantha.' His father dropped the name with the flair of a magician pulling a rabbit out of a hat.

'Samantha...' Leo repeated slowly.

'Little Sammy Wilson,' Harold expanded.

'You know who I'm talking about. She would be perfect for the part!'

'You want me to involve *Samantha Wilson* in a far-fetched charade to win custody of Adele?'

'It makes perfect sense.'

'In whose world?'

'Don't be rude, son!' Harold reprimanded with an unusual amount of authority.

'Does she know about this? Have you two been plotting this crazy scheme behind my back?' Leo was aghast. His father had clearly taken leave of his senses.

'I haven't mentioned a word of this to her,' Harold admitted. 'Well, you know that she only manages to get to Salcombe on weekends...'

'No, I didn't. Why would I?'

'You will have to broach the subject with her. You can be very persuasive and I don't see why you wouldn't bring those considerable skills to bear on this. It's not as though I ask favours of you as a general rule. I think it's the very least you can do, son. I would so love to know Adele is safe and cared for and we both know that Gail would make as bad a grandparent as her daughter made a parent. I would spend the remainder of my days fearing for what might happen to the girl...'

'Gail might be many things,' Leo returned

drily, 'but aren't you over-egging the pudding here?'

His father breezed over the interruption. 'And you would condemn a child to a future with a woman of that calibre? *We both know the rumours about her...*' His eyes, when they met Leo's, were filled with sadness. 'I can't force you but I'm very much afraid that I... Well, what would be the point of my living...?'

Samantha hadn't been in her tiny rented flat for more than half an hour before she heard the insistent buzz of her doorbell and she grimaced with annoyance.

She had too much to do to waste time on a cold-caller. Or, worse, her neighbour from the flat upstairs, who had a habit of randomly showing up around this hour, a little after six in the evening, for wine with someone too polite and too soft-hearted to turn her away.

Samantha had spent many hours listening to her neighbour discuss her latest boyfriend or weep over a broken heart that would never be mended.

Right now, she simply had too much to do.

Too much homework from her eight-year-old charges to mark. Too many lessons to prepare. Too much red tape with Ofsted to get through.

Not to mention the bank, who had been politely reminding her mother for the past three months that the mortgage hadn't been paid.

But whoever was at the door wasn't about to go away, not if the insistent finger on the button was anything to go by.

Sweeping the stack of exercise books off her lap and onto the little coffee table by the side of her chair and plunging her feet into her cosy bedroom slippers, she was working out which negative response, depending on who was at the door, she would be delivering so that her evening remained uninterrupted.

She yanked open the door and her mouth fell open. Literally. She stood there like a stranded goldfish, eyes like saucers, because the last person she ever, in a million years, had expected to see was standing in front of her.

Or rather lounging, his long, muscular body indolently leaning against the door frame, his hands thrust into the pockets of his black cashmere coat.

It had been several weeks since she had seen Leo Morgan-White.

He had nodded to her from across the width of his father's massive drawing room, which had been crowded with at least three dozen locals, all friends from the village where his father and her mother lived. Harold was a popular member of the community and his annual Christmas party was something of an event on the local calendar.

She hadn't even spoken to Leo that night. He'd been there with a leggy brunette who, in the depths of winter, had been wearing something very bright and very short, garnering attention from every single male in the room.

'Have I come at a bad time?'

He'd taken the bait. Sly old fox that his father was, Leo had been persuaded into doing the unthinkable by the threat of ill health and a return of the depression that had dogged his father for years and from which he was only recently surfacing.

Of course, Harold genuinely and truly wanted Adele close to him and safe and, of course, he truly believed, and was probably spot on, that Gail would turn out to be a horrendous influence on her five-year-old granddaughter, but when he had pulled the ill-health-so-what's-the-point-of-carrying-on? threat from the hat Leo had confessed himself to be beaten.

So here he was, two days later, with the soon-to-be object of his desire standing in front of him in some dull grey outfit and a pair of ridiculous, brightly coloured bedroom slippers.

'Leo?' Sammy blinked and wondered whether it was possible for stress to induce very realistic hallucinations. 'What do you want? How did you find out where I live? What on earth are you doing here?'

'Lots of questions, and I'll answer them just as soon as you invite me in.'

Struck by a sudden thought, Sammy paled and stared up at him. 'Has something happened? Is your dad all right?' She was finding it very difficult to think but then the wretched man had always had that effect on her. Something about his devastatingly good looks. He was just so...*so much larger than life.*

Taller, more striking, with the rakish, swarthy sexiness of a pirate. Next to him, the rest of the male population always seemed to pale in comparison and, considering the long, long line of women he had run through over the years, she wasn't the only one who thought so.

Unlike that long, long line of women, though, she knew better than to let all that drop-dead male sexiness get to her.

She still cringed in shame when she thought back to that awful incident years ago. She'd had gone along to a party at *the big house*, as everyone in the village called the Morgan-White mansion up on the hill.

The place had been teeming with people. It had been a birthday bash for Leo and half the world seemed to be there. Heaven only knew why she'd been invited but she imagined that it had been something of a pity invite and, whilst she had cringed at the thought of going, she had been encouraged by the fact that several of the locals had also been on the guest list so she wouldn't be a complete fish out of water. She'd spent ages choosing just the right dress. She'd only spotted him from a distance later, when she had been standing in the garden and, miracle of miracles, he had shown up right next to her and they had chatted for what had seemed like ages. He'd torn himself away from his gilded crowd and Sammy had been on cloud nine until, late in the evening, a very tall, very blonde girl had broken free from the group and confronted her just outside the marquee which had been erected in the garden.

'You're making a bloody fool of yourself,' she'd hissed, words slurring from too much free champagne. 'Can't you see that Leo is never, and I mean *never*, going to give you the time of day? You may have grown up next to him but you're poor, you're fat and you're boring. You're making a laughing stock of yourself.'

Her infatuation had died fast. Since then, watching off and on from the sidelines, she had come to see just how repulsive his approach to women was. He picked them up and then, when he'd got what he wanted and boredom began setting in, he dumped them without a backward glance and moved on.

Romantic at heart, with a core of firmly held family values, Sammy marvelled that she could ever have looked twice at someone like Leo. But, then again, she'd been young and he'd been crazily good-looking.

'He's been better. Are you going to invite me in or are we going to have this conversation here?'

'I suppose you can come in.'

Great start, Leo thought wryly. *A very auspicious beginning to what's intended to be the relationship of a lifetime.*

He hadn't thought about how she was going to react to his proposition but he didn't expect too much protesting. He was, after all, bringing a great deal of money to the table and, as everyone knew, money talked a lot louder than words.

Anne Wilson, Samantha's mother, was a close friend of his father's and had been since Leo's mother had fallen ill and Anne, a nurse at the local hospital, had gone beyond the call of duty to help out. Their bond had strengthened over the years as she had proved to be a solid rock upon whom his father had often leaned, particularly after his acrimonious divorce from Georgia.

It was no surprise then that Anne had confided in Harold about her ill health and the money problems she was having with the bank because she had been forced to quit her job. Though Harold had offered to give her the money, and, when that hadn't worked, to lend it to her, she had refused.

'So...' Sammy folded her arms and stared at him almost before he had shut the door behind him. 'What have you come here for?' He was so good-looking that she could barely look at him without blushing.

Leo's fabulous looks had to do with far more than just the arrangement of his features. Yes, he was indecently perfect, from the long, dark, thick lashes that shielded equally dark eyes and the straight, arrogant nose to the sensuous curve of his mouth. Yes, he had the toned, lean, six-foot-two-inch frame of an athlete and the lazy grace of some kind of predatory jungle animal, but he also generated an impression of power that was frankly mesmerising.

'Are you always so welcoming to visitors?' Leo drawled, ignoring her bristling hostility to shrug off his coat, which he proceeded to dump on the coat hook by the front door.

The house had clearly been made into flats, each with a separate entrance and, from the looks of it, on the cheap. Too much door-slamming and the whole structure would collapse like a house of cards.

'I happen to be very busy at the moment,' Sammy said shortly. She led the way into the sitting room and gestured to the mound of exercise books which she had been about to look at.

He sat himself in a chair. He had come to visit for reasons she couldn't begin to understand and she was furious with herself for the silly heat that was pouring through her.

She was as awkward as he recalled. He'd never spoken to her without getting the feeling that she would much rather have been somewhere else. He'd never really paid a huge amount of attention to her appearance in the past, simply absorbing the impression that she didn't dress to impress, but now that she was going to be the love of his life he couldn't help but notice that she *really* had mastered the art of not making an effort.

Accustomed to women who bent over backwards to show off flawless bodies, who devoted unreasonable amounts of time to their appearance, he was weirdly disconcerted by someone who didn't seem to give a hoot. He stared at her narrowly, recognising that, despite the appalling dress sense and the mop of blond hair that had been piled on top of her head and secured with a fluorescent elastic band, there was a certain pretty appeal to her heart-shaped face. Plus she had amazing eyes. Huge, cornflower blue with long lashes.

'I take it you're not interested in pleasantries, so shall I skip past the bit where I ask you how you are and what you've been up to recently?'

'Do you care how I am and what I've been up to recently?'

'You should sit down, Sammy. The reason I'm here is because I have something of a complicated favour to ask. If you insist on hearing me out on your feet, then you're going to have aching calves by the time I'm through.'

'A favour? What are you talking about? I don't see how I could possibly help you out with anything.'

'Sit down. No, better still…why don't you offer me a glass of wine? Or a cup of coffee?'

Sammy resisted scowling. By nature, she was a kind-hearted woman who would never have dreamed of being downright rude to anyone she knew, but something about Leo always got her back up. She'd long ago written him off as too rich, too good-looking and too arrogant, and the way he had settled into her flat and was proceeding to order her about was only hardening her attitude.

She would quite have liked to have asked him politely to clear off.

As though reading her mind, Leo raised his eyebrows and subjected her to a long, appraising look that made her go red.

'Okay,' he drawled, 'I'll cut to the chase, shall I?' He shifted slightly, reached inside his trouser pocket and withdrew a small box which he dumped on the table in front of him. 'I'm here to ask you to marry me.'

CHAPTER TWO

SAMMY BLINKED AND then folded her arms, body as rigid as a plank of wood. Anger was bubbling up inside her. After one glance at the navy blue box he had dumped on the table, she hadn't deigned to give it a second look.

'Is this some kind of joke?' she asked coldly.

'Do I look like the kind of man who would show up on a woman's doorstep and propose marriage as a joke?'

'I have no idea, Leo. I don't know what kind of person you are.' Aside, she thought furiously, from the obvious.

'Open the box.'

Sammy eyed it with a guarded expression and did nothing of the sort. But her fingers were twitching and, uttering a soft, impatient curse under her breath, she reached down and flipped open the lid.

An engagement ring nestled on a deep blue velvet cushion. The exquisite solitaire diamond blinked at her and she blinked back at it, utterly dumbfounded. Her hand was shaking as she placed the box, still open, back on the table and moved to sit down on the chair facing him.

'What the heck is going on here, Leo? You can't possibly be serious. You show up here with an engagement ring, asking me to marry you. Something's wrong. What is it? Is that ring even real?'

'Oh, it's a hundred per cent real. And guess what? You get to keep it when this is all over.'

Sammy's head was swimming. Less than an hour ago, she was a stressed out primary school teacher with a stack of exercise books to mark. Now, she was the main character in some weird parallel universe story with a sexy billionaire sitting on one of her chairs and an engagement ring in front of her.

Nothing about this scenario was making any sense.

'When *what's* all over?' she asked as she tried to make sense of the situation and came up blank.

Leo sighed. Maybe he should have forewarned her but what would have been the point? She would still have been utterly bewildered. Much better that he was sitting in front of her so that he could explain the situation face-to-face.

If she couldn't believe that this was happening then they were roughly on the same page.

Beyond the fact that the words *will you marry me* had never featured in any scenario he had ever envisaged for his future, he certainly would never have chosen Samantha Wilson as the recipient of his proposal.

He had met the woman over the years in countless different situations and he had been left with the impression of someone so background as to be practically invisible. She'd never been rude to him. She had always answered his questions politely, barely meeting his eyes before scuttling away as soon as she could. Aside from one conversation years ago. A conversation lodged at the back of his brain... But, after that, he had met her again— had tried to engage her attention—and nothing. He had no idea whether she had a boyfriend or not, whether she had a social life or not, whether she had hobbies or not.

In his world, where women strutted around like flamboyant peacocks, she was the equivalent of a sparrow. Perfect, of course, for the job at hand but hardly the sort of woman he would ever have looked at twice in *that* way.

'I suppose you know about Sean and his wife,' Leo began.

She nodded slowly. 'I'm sorry. You have my condolences. It was a horrible end for both of them. What on earth would have persuaded Sean to take *flying lessons,* of all things? And to have flown solo in bad weather with Louise, without his instructor... It beggars belief. But I'm so sorry.'

'No need for the sorrow or the condolences—' he waved aside '—I wasn't close to Sean so I can't say his absence is going to leave a big hole in my life.'

'That's very honest of you.'

She was looking at him with those huge, surprisingly riveting blue, blue eyes and, while her voice was perfectly serious, Leo couldn't help but suspect a thread of sarcasm underlying her remark. She'd never struck him as the sarcastic type.

'I suppose you're also aware that my father has been extremely upset that Sean's daughter, whom he considers his granddaughter, remains in Australia as a ward of her maternal grandmother.'

'It's a shame, but I'm sure she'll be allowed over to visit your dad in time, once she's a bit older. Look, Leo, I still don't see what this has to do with me or—' her eyes flicked down to the box burning a hole on the table in front of her '—or that engagement ring.'

'When Sean and Louise died, it was presumed that the child would be sent over here to live with me. Louise was an only child from a difficult background, without any extended family who could take Adele under their wing and Louise's mother also had a somewhat... colourful history.'

'I know there have been rumours...'

'My father receives monthly requests from her for handouts and that is in addition to the money he continued to send to Sean over the years, well after his divorce from Sean's mother was finalised.'

'Your dad has a soft heart,' Sammy said warmly.

'A soft heart is only a small step away from being a soft touch,' Leo muttered and she frowned disapprovingly at him.

'I'm sure the money he sent over was really useful...'

'I'm sure it was,' Leo responded drily. 'The question is, useful to whom? But no matter. That's history. What we're dealing with is the present, which brings me to the subject of the engagement ring...' Admittedly, he had sprung this on her and had expected nothing but shock. Horror, however, hadn't entered the equation because, whether the engagement was fake or not, he couldn't think of a single woman who wouldn't have been thrilled to see a diamond like that and to know that it was destined for *her* finger.

Right now, the woman sitting in front of him was glancing down at the box with a moue of distaste, as though looking at something that could prove infectious in a nasty way.

'My father has recently received an unpleasant email suggesting that Adele, against all common sense and certainly not in her best interests, may end up remaining in Australia with Sean's mother-in-law. The woman has clearly decided that it makes sense financially for her to hang on to Adele because, as long as she has the child in her custody, she will continue to receive money from my father, which, incidentally, is actually money from me. You may or may not know that his writing has been off the boil for a long time. The family company is doing well but I would rather not be financially embroiled with this woman forever.'

'I'm just wondering what all of this has to do with me,' Sammy confessed.

This had to be the longest conversation in recent years that she had ever had with the man and she was mortified because the cool composure she was at pains to display was at vibrant odds with what she was feeling. She certainly wasn't cool and composed inside. In fact, she was all over the place.

Her senses were on full alert and she didn't fully understand *why*.

Surely she was mature enough not to turn into a dithering wreck simply because she happened to be in the company of a man who was too attractive for his own good? She was a working woman, a teacher, with heaps of responsibility, someone with enough life experience behind her to recognise Leo for the man he really was as opposed to the one-dimensional, gorgeous cardboard cut-out who had once turned her silly teenage head...

Except...

Maybe her life experience was sorely lacking in a certain vital area. Maybe that was why just looking at him was making her skin tingle.

She had plenty of experience in caring for her mother, as she had been doing for the past year and a half. She knew all about communicating with doctors and hospitals and nurses and making her voice heard because her mother, although she had been a nurse herself, had been swallowed up with fear and confusion. She had needed someone strong to lean on and that person had been her, Sammy. And she had plenty of experience under her belt of taking charge, of controlling unruly primary school children until they were as meek as little lambs.

She had argued with bank managers and spent hours trying to balance the books and had exhausted herself with pep talks to her mother, convincing her that the cottage was safe even though the mortgage payments had fallen behind.

And, through it all, she had done her best to hang on to her sense of humour and her sense of perspective.

But there was that whole other area where she had no experience at all.

A vast, blurry, opaque space where she was a stranger because, despite having had two serious boyfriends, she had yet to test the sexual waters.

They had both been attractive and she'd liked them very much. In fact, they'd ticked all the boxes in her head in terms of suitability and yet…she just hadn't *fancied* them enough to go the whole way.

She and Pete had broken up over a year and a half ago, and since then she had resigned herself to the fact that there was probably something wrong with her. Some faulty gene in her make-up. Maybe it was because there had been no father figure in her life since she had been a kid, yet, even to her, that argument made no sense.

So she'd long stopped analysing the whys and maybes.

She hadn't taken into account that her lack of experience in that small, stupid area, *insignificant in the big scheme of things*, might have left her vulnerable to a man like Leo, with his sexy, spectacular good looks and that lazy, assessing charm that oozed from every pore.

'Sean had the foresight, strangely, to leave something of a will,' he was saying now, 'a scrap of paper signed by a friend. In it, he indicated that, should anything happen to him, I should take guardianship of the child. I'm sure,' Leo elaborated with scrupulous honesty, 'that that particular light bulb idea had something to do with my financial worth.'

'That's very cynical of you.' Sammy was still smarting from the realisation that while two perfectly good boyfriends hadn't been able to get to her, this utterly inappropriate man seemingly could. At least if the crazy somersaulting in her stomach was anything to go by.

'So I'm cynical.' He shrugged and stared at her. 'It's a trait that's always stood me in good stead.'

'If Sean meant for you to have Adele, then what's the problem?'

'The problem is the harridan of a grandmother who's decided to hire a lawyer to argue the case that I'm unfit to be the child's guardian. A scrap of paper, she maintains, counts for nothing, especially considering my former stepbrother lived with a stash of alcohol and drugs within easy reach.'

Sammy didn't say anything and Leo frowned because he could read what she was thinking as clearly as if her thoughts had been transcribed in neon lettering across her forehead.

'The woman isn't equipped to raise Adele,' he grated. 'Even if she had been an angel in human form, it would still be a big ask for her to take over the role of looking after an energetic five-year-old child. Had I felt that she might conceivably be mentally fit for the job then I'd back off, but she isn't. At any rate, my father is distraught at this turn of events.'

'He's always mourned the fact that he never got to see her. He talked about that a lot to me and Mum.'

'Yes, well…' Somehow that simple statement of fact, which came as no shock at all to Leo, indicated a familiarity that was a little unsettling. 'Here's where we're nearing the crux of the matter. I've been accused of having too many women and spending too much time out of the country.' He raked his fingers through his hair and gestured in a manner that was redolent with frustration and impatience.

Sammy remained silent because, from all accounts, those were some pretty accurate accusations.

'Well...' she finally said. 'I suppose there might be some truth in that. From everything I've heard, I mean, that's to say...'

'Please—' Leo scowled darkly '—don't let good manners stand in the way of saying what's on your mind. I take it the rumours about me have come from my father?'

'No!'

'Do you three just sit around gossiping about my love life?'

'No! You've got the wrong end of the stick.'

'Have I? From the sounds of it, once my father has finished lamenting the fact that he's been denied access to his "granddaughter," he brings out the tea and biscuits and gets down to the gritty business of discussing my personal life!'

'It's not like that at all!' Sammy was mortified at the picture he was painting. 'Your dad mentioned ages ago that he wished he saw more of you and that you worked too hard. He worries about your health, that's all.'

'I've never had a day's illness in my life.'

'Working too hard can bring on all sorts of problems,' Sammy said, fidgeting, her colour high. 'Stress can be a killer. That's what worries your dad.'

'That being the case,' Leo drawled, 'he must know that I'm in no danger of collapsing from working too hard or being too stressed because I have my safety valves in the form of my very diverting playmates.'

Sammy's breath caught in her throat, which was suddenly so dry that she could barely get her words out.

It struck Leo that those very diverting playmates were going to have to take a back seat, at least for the time being, and he was a little surprised that he didn't feel more gutted at the prospect. He was a highly sexual man with a very energetic libido, but recently, beautiful and obliging women who were always willing to go the extra mile for him had left him dissatisfied.

His palate was jaded.

Perhaps now was a very good time to indulge in a fake engagement with a woman he had precisely nothing in common with. A couple of months pretending to be in love with someone who didn't stand a chance of rousing his interest might be just the ticket. He would resume life with renewed vigour and things would be back to normal. And a bout of celibacy never killed anyone.

'Which—' he brought the conversation neatly back to the point at hand '—brings us back to the problem. I don't, according to my father, make a credible guardian with my reputation, and I will be under scrutiny because I will be travelling to Melbourne to sort this situation out. Eyes will be on me. I need credibility— and here is where you come in. I need a fiancée to show my stability to the Melbourne courts and he's suggested that you would be perfect for the part.'

Sammy stared at him. So that was what all of this was about. The ring. The proposal. It was so preposterous that she was torn between bursting into manic laughter and propelling him out of her flat.

She did neither. Instead, she said, 'You've got to be kidding, right?'

'As I've already told you, I have better things

to do than show up here for a laugh. This is no joke, Samantha.' He leaned forward and looked at her with utter seriousness. 'My father refuses to accept that he may never see Adele. The fact that Sean was his stepson for a short period of time rather than his own flesh and blood and that any tenuous family connection they might have once had ended when he and Georgia divorced makes not a scrap of difference to him, but then he's that kind of man, as I expect you already know. He sees this as his last chance to do something about the situation and he can't understand any hesitancy on my part to leap aboard the plan.'

'I'm not going to go with you to the other side of the world so that I can pretend to be your fiancée, Leo!' Agitated, Sammy leapt to her feet and began pacing the room. Her thoughts were all over the place and her body was burning.

'Why would you want me to be your *fake fiancée*, anyway?' She spun round to look at him, hands on hips. 'Why don't you just pick one of those women from your little black book? You have enough to choose from! Every time I open a tabloid I seem to see you somewhere in the gossip columns with a glamour model hanging on to you for dear life.'

Leo's eyebrows shot up and he gave her a

slow, curling smile. 'Follow me in the tabloids, do you?'

'Trust you to put that spin on it,' Sammy muttered under her breath, which seemed to amuse him further. 'I won't do it,' she said flatly. 'You can have your pick of any woman you want so go ahead and pick one of them.'

'But none of them will do,' Leo said smoothly and Sammy paused to frown.

'Why not?'

He looked at her for a long while in perfect silence and it didn't take her long to get the message.

'Too glamorous,' Sammy said slowly, while she pointlessly wished the ground would open and swallow her, disgorging her somewhere on the other side of the world. 'You need someone plain and average, someone who would give the right image of a responsible other half, able to take on a young child.'

Accustomed to telling it like it was, Leo had the grace to flush. 'The women I date would be inappropriate—' he smoothed over the un-varnished bluntness of her statement '—it has nothing to do with looks.'

'It has *everything* to do with looks,' Sammy retorted, her voice shaking. 'I want you to leave. Right now. I'd love to be able to help your father but I draw the line at being manipulated into playing the part of your dreary fiancée so that you can try and fool the authorities in Australia into believing that you're a halfway decent guy with a few responsible bones in his body!'

Leo was outraged at the barrage of insults contained in that outburst. *Halfway decent guy? A few responsible bones?*

He stayed right where he was, a solid mass of sheer physical strength. He wasn't going anywhere and she would be more than welcome to try and budge him if she wanted. She wouldn't get far.

'Leave!' she snapped.

'Sit,' he returned.

'How dare you come into my house and… and…?'

'I'm not done with this conversation.' Leo looked at her steadily and she gritted her teeth in impotent fury.

There was no way she could force him out. He was way too big and far too strong. *And he knew it.*

'There's nothing else to say,' she told him in a frozen voice. 'There's no way you could persuade me to go along with your scheme.' Those cruelly delivered words from when she was a teenager had rushed back towards her with the force of a freight train. As an awkward, self-conscious adolescent she hadn't been his type and as a twenty-six-year-old woman she *still* wasn't his type…

She didn't care because, as it happened, he was no more her type than she was his, but it still hurt to have it shoved down her throat.

'Sure about that?'

Sammy didn't bother to answer. Her arms were still folded, her face was still a mask of resentment, her legs were still squarely apart as she continued to stare down at him.

He couldn't have looked more relaxed.

She marvelled how someone who adored his father so much could actually be so odious, but then he was a high-flying businessman with no morals to speak of when it came to women so why was she surprised?

'One hundred per cent sure,' she threw at him.

'Because I haven't just popped along here to ask a favour without bringing something to the table…'

'I don't see what you could possibly *bring to the table* that could be of any interest to me.'

'I like the moral high ground,' he murmured in a voice that left her in no doubt that the moral high ground was the very last thing he liked.

'But, in my experience, moral high grounds usually have their foundations built on sand. Why don't you sit down and finish hearing me out? If, at the end of what I have to say, you're still adamant that you want no part of this arrangement, then so be it. My father will be bitterly disappointed, but that's life. He won't be able to accuse me of not trying.'

Sammy hesitated. He wasn't going anywhere. The wretched man was going to stay put until he had said what he had come to say—the whole speech and nothing but the whole speech.

Why waste time arguing?

She perched on the edge of the chair and waited for him to continue.

He was truly a beautiful human being, she thought. All raven-black hair and piercing black eyes and fantastically chiselled features. It was hardly the time to be thinking this, but she just couldn't help herself.

Was it any wonder that there weren't many women between the ages of twenty-one and ninety-one who wouldn't have crashed into a lamp post to grab a second look?

She tried to imagine one of those women he dated trying to pass herself off as a suitable bride-to-be and, whilst it certainly worked from the gorgeous couple aspect, the whole thing fell apart the second a little girl was put in the equation.

'Your mother hasn't been well,' Leo said quietly. 'I'm sorry that this is the first time I've... commiserated.'

'She's going to be fine.' Sammy tilted her chin at an angle but, as always when she thought about her mother, the tears were never very far away.

'Yes. I've been told the chemotherapy has been successful and that the tumour has shrunk considerably. You must be relieved.'

'I don't understand what my mother has to do with any of this.'

'Then I'll come straight to the point.' He hadn't felt a single qualm when he had considered using money as leverage in this bartering process. This was the world he occupied. It was always a quid pro quo system.

Now, however, he was assailed by a sudden attack of conscience. Something about the way her eyes were glistening and the slight wobble of her full pink lips.

No wonder she and his father got on like a house on fire, he thought. They were equally sentimental.

It was yet another reason why the arrangement would work for them because her emotionalism was guaranteed to get on his nerves. There would be no chance of any lines between them getting blurred.

'It would appear,' he said heavily, 'that there's a problem with the mortgage repayments on the house your mother's in.'

'How do you know that?'

'The same way you seem to have great insight into *my* personal life,' he returned coolly. 'Our respective parents seem to do an awful lot of confidence sharing. At any rate, the fact is that there is a real threat of the bank closing on the house if the late payments aren't made soon.'

'I've been to see the bank.' Sammy's skin burnt because she hated this sliver of her life being exposed. It was none of his business. 'Mum's had to give up her job, with all the treatment, and I've had to move to a different, more expensive place here because the landlord in my last place wanted to sell. Plus there've been all the additional costs of travelling back and forth every weekend, sometimes during the week, as well. I haven't been able to contribute as much as I would have liked to the finances but they said they understood at the bank.'

'Banks,' Leo informed her kindly, 'have

never been noted for their understanding policies. They're not charitable organisations. The most sympathetic bank manager, under instruction, will foreclose on a house with very little prior warning. I also appreciate that it costs you dearly to be working so far from your mother at a time when she needs you to be on hand.'

'Your dad had no right to tell you all that stuff...'

'Was any of it confidential information?'

Sammy didn't reply. No, none of it was confidential, although sitting here right now and listening to him explain her life to her made her think that perhaps it ought to have been.

Naturally, he would never understand what it might be like to really have to count pennies and to struggle against all odds to meet the bills. He had been born into money and, even in the village, his name was legend as the guy who had built his own empire and turned it into a gold mine.

'Didn't think so. I know he offered to give your mother money to help her out of this little sticky patch but she refused.'

'And I don't blame her,' Sammy said, her cheeks dully flushed. 'There's such a thing as pride.'

'Yes. It usually comes before a fall. No matter. I get it. But the fact remains that you are both facing considerable financial challenges, so here is my proposal.' He allowed anticipation to settle before continuing. 'In return for your services, so to speak, I will settle all outstanding money owing on your mother's house.' He raised one hand as though she had interrupted although, in fact, she couldn't have uttered a word if she'd wanted to. She was mesmerised by him. By the movement of his mouth as he spoke, by the steady flex of muscle discernible under his clothing, by the elegance of his gestures and the commanding timbre of his voice.

'Furthermore,' he continued, 'I understand that your dream is to work freelance. Your degree was in graphic art and, whilst you do as much freelance work as you can get your hands on, it's impossible to make the jump because you need to have a steady income.'

Sammy paled. 'Now *that*,' she burst out, 'definitely *was* confidential!'

'Is that some of your work over there?' Leo nodded to a desk by the window and the layers of stiff board piled to one side. Without giving her time to answer, far less swoop to the rescue of the job she was currently trying to find the time to work on, he began rifling through the illustrations she had so far completed while she remained frozen to the spot, mouth open.

'They're good.' Leo turned to face her. He was genuinely impressed. 'Don't glare at me as though I've exposed state secrets,' he said drily. 'This is the second part of my proposition. Not only am I willing to settle the debt on your mother's house but I will also get builders in to construct a suitable extension at the back of the property.'

'A suitable extension?' Sammy said faintly.

'To accommodate this—' he gestured to the desk and the artwork he had just been rifling through '—you setting up your own business where your mother is. No more commuting. No more wasting money on rent you can barely afford. And not only that, Sammy, but I will immediately instigate a steady income that will cover the transition period between you giving up your teaching post here and establishing yourself in your field.'

Sammy was beginning to sympathise with anyone unfortunate enough to have been run over by a steamroller. 'It's a ridiculous suggestion...' she protested, but she could hear telltale signs of weakness in her voice. 'Go to Melbourne...? Pretend to be engaged to you...? It's crazy.'

'Perhaps if you just had yourself to consider,' Leo pointed out with inexorable, irrefutable logic, 'you could spend the next hour talking about your pride or maybe just chuck me out of here immediately, but this isn't just about you. Your mother's future is involved here, as well.'

'And it's not fair of you to drag her into this.'

'Who said that life was fair? If life was fair, that harridan wouldn't be trying to hang on to a granddaughter she probably doesn't even want for the sake of what she thinks she might be able to coerce out of me. Agree to my proposal and I could have builders at the house first thing in the morning to ascertain what needs to be done. All you would have to do is hand your notice in and look forward to a life of no stress, close to your mother.'

Sammy thought of the amount of time she had spent trying to get the books to balance and trying to work out how many more hours she could put into her illustrations so that more income could be generated.

'What happens if you get custody of the little girl?' she questioned eventually, forcibly tearing herself away from that stress-free vision he had been dangling in front of her.

'I'll cross that bridge when I get to it. I can afford the very best day care, the very best schools and during the holidays there will be the option of spending time by the sea with my father.'

Sammy's brow pleated and Leo felt he should jump in before she began testing the moral high ground once again.

'I'm going to give you forty-eight hours to think about my proposition. Time for you to work out the nitty-gritty details and break the glad tidings to your mother, although there's a fair to middling chance that she already knows that I'm here with you right now, thanks to my father. I'll leave the engagement ring here. Try not to misplace it.' He told her how much it had cost and her mouth fell open. 'No point getting something cheap and nasty. You'd be surprised what a nosy reporter can spot through a tele-photo lens. If you agree to this, no one must think that it's anything but genuine.'

'I may not agree to anything.'

'Your call.' He shrugged. 'Just think about the trade-off.' He stood up and glanced at his watch to find that far more time had gone by than he'd expected. 'One more thing to con-sider…'

Sammy had scrambled to her feet but she was still keeping her distance. She wasn't going to touch this offer with a bargepole. Was she?

It smacked of blackmail and surely any form of deceit, however well intended, was a bad thing...

'What's that?' She eyed him warily.

'You asked why you're perfect for this...arrangement.' He kept his eyes fixed on her face as he began putting on his coat. 'You understand the rules. I don't mean the rules that involve pretending—I mean the rules that dictate that this isn't for real. You're not one of my women who might get it into their heads that a fake engagement might turn into a real engagement.'

'No. I'm not.' *Because there was no way he would ever consider getting engaged for real to someone like her.* She'd never wanted to slap someone as much as she had spent the past couple of hours wanting to slap him.

'So we're on the same page,' Leo drawled, tilting his head at her. 'Always a good thing. I'll be in touch for your decision.'

'You're going to traipse all the way back here...?'

'Oh, no. I'll call you. And no need to give me your mobile number. I already have it.' He allowed himself a mocking half smile. 'I look forward to talking to you soon...my wife-to-be.'

CHAPTER THREE

HE WAS SO damned sure of himself!

Sammy had spent the next forty-eight hours fuming. Her ability for recall was obviously world-class because she could remember every detail of Leo's visit and every fleeting expression on his face as he had laid out his proposal.

The fact that he had waltzed in with an engagement ring said it all. He hadn't expected to leave her flat without a satisfactory conclusion to his offer.

He hadn't arrived on her doorstep to ask a favour of her. He had arrived on her doorstep to blackmail her into helping him out. He'd held all the trump cards and he'd known that she would have been unable to refuse him.

As he had cleverly pointed out, her agreement to go along with him would make a world of difference to her mother and would relieve her of the constant low-level stress of worrying about the house and the unpaid remainder of mortgage. The fact that she would also have her daughter around and at hand for as long as was necessary had been just another bonus factor.

The deal was done before he'd issued her a time limit in which to make her mind up. He'd even correctly predicted that her mother had been well aware of his proposition so there had been no shock or surprise when Sammy had called to discuss it with her.

And now here she was, waiting for him to show up like a sixteen-year-old nervously counting the minutes until her date showed up to take her to the prom.

Except Leo was no normal date and her nerves did not stem from eager excitement.

She saw his car when it had almost come to a stop outside the house and she hurriedly flew back from the window and then waited until she heard the buzz of the doorbell.

She had dressed in defiant combat mode—literally. A pair of combat trousers, a green long-sleeved thermal vest, over which she had on her warmest army-green jumper, trainers and her waterproof coat with its very sensible furry hood.

She pulled open the door and, for a second,

the breath caught in her throat as she stared up at him.

It was freezing. Sleet was falling, the skies the colour of lead. Yet, for all the discomfort of the weather, Leo still managed to look expensive, elegant and sexy in black jeans, a black jumper and a tan trench coat.

'You're not wearing the engagement ring' was the first thing he said.

'I didn't think there was any need to stick it on just yet.'

'Every need. The loving couple wants to advertise their love, not hide it away like a shameful secret. Where is it?'

'It's in my bag.'

'Then I suggest you fetch it out and put it on. And there's something else.' He eyed her outfit. 'I'm under strict orders not to tell you this, but there's a little surprise reception waiting for us when we get to my father's house.'

Sammy, in the act of rustling through her backpack to locate the box with the engagement ring, froze. *Surprise reception?*'

'My father's idea. You know he's inclined towards sentimentality.'

'This is a *fake* engagement, Leo! It's going to last until Adele is over here and then there's going to be a *fake* break-up!'

'Believe me, I told him that, but he said the whole thing wouldn't sit right without some kind of celebration marking the big event. He's got a point. Over the years, he hasn't exactly been reticent when it's come to voicing his desire to see me married off. After our last conversation, he confessed that he's done a bit of complaining to his cronies at the bowling club and the gardening club and all those other clubs he's joined, that he'd like nothing more than to have a wonderful daughter-in-law. Apparently, it's what my mother would have wanted. It seems he had chatty conversations with her every so often and she told him that she was keen to see me settle down. I have no doubt that that little titbit has also been discussed over fertiliser tips for the roses. It would seem odd if his dearest wish were to come to pass and he kept it to himself,' Leo told her flatly. 'His friends would be mortally offended and, worse, some might suspect that he was making the whole thing up.' He glanced across at her. 'And, like I said, there can be no room for speculation about this.'

'It just doesn't seem right, Leo.'

Leo clicked his tongue impatiently. 'We wouldn't be doing this if Gail weren't so patently unfit to be in charge of the child.'

'You should stop calling her *the child*. It makes you seem cold and unfeeling.'

'We're getting off-topic,' Leo drawled. He held up a bag, which she hadn't noticed him holding, and dangled it in front of her. 'Little present here for you.'

'Huh?'

'Outfit for the engagement party you don't know about. I thought a dress might suit the occasion a little more than jeans and a jumper, which I somehow knew you'd greet me in. Little did I know that you would go one step further and dress for all-out war. And don't argue with me on this one, Sammy. Put it on and let's get going.'

Sammy bristled but he wasn't going to budge and she snatched the bag from him. Pink, with fancy black lettering, clearly designer. Clearly the sort of thing he liked seeing women in, which would be just the sort of thing she wouldn't want to wear. 'Bossy,' she muttered, heading inside.

'And another small point.' He stayed her. 'We're supposed to be engaged. People who are engaged are generally happy and pleased to be in one another's company. Sniping and snarling is going to have to stop. Do I make myself clear?'

Sammy went beetroot-red. 'I feel as though

I've been forced into doing this,' she admitted truthfully. 'And now I'm being ordered to get dolled up.'

'I'm no more a fan of deception than you are, believe it or not. I've had to rearrange vast swathes of my working life to accommodate the joy of being engaged and getting out to Australia to sort out a woman who has been a thorn in my side since Sean died. Throw into the mix that I find myself coping with someone who seems to have perfected the art of moaning, and you get the picture that I'm not exactly a willing participant in this situation! And, just for the record, you should try thinking about all the upsides of being *forced into doing this*. Life is going to be very sweet for you from here on in. If stress causes ill health then you should be fighting fit for a hundred years! And you might just like the dress I brought for you. I'll wait here while you put it on.' He glanced at his watch pointedly and lounged against the wall in we're-on-a-deadline-here mode.

She had expected small, tight and borderline tarty. It was what the women he went out with wore. That was his preferred style of dress for a woman. So she was startled to find herself stepping into the most beautiful soft, dusky pink woollen dress imaginable. Long-sleeved, knee-length, simple cowl neck, it was soft and demure and fitted her like a glove and she hated to admit it but she loved it.

She also hated to admit that it challenged her view of him as a womanising playboy who had got his own way on this, secured his deal with her and now wanted to dress her up like the sort of doll he imagined would pass muster on his arm in the role of fiancée. This dress was classy and it had been, she was forced to concede, a thoughtful purchase. He had actually considered how she would react in her scruffy clothes at a surprise gathering and had preempted her embarrassment by providing her with the perfect outfit.

She was much subdued when she joined him back in the hallway, where he was still lounging against the wall, scrolling through his cell phone.

Brilliant eyes shielded as he looked at her, Leo straightened and briskly congratulated her on the quick change of clothes.

Not a word about how she looked, she thought with a flare of disappointment, which she immediately quelled because *none of this was real*.

'Do I look a little more presentable?' Had she actually meant to ask that?

'Definite step up from the war zone look,'

he murmured. He opened the car door for her and she stepped inside. 'Now all we need is a smile now and again and some lingering, tender glances and you'll be the complete package.'

'You're very cold, aren't you?' She absently thought that he was truly breathtakingly handsome. 'And your dad is such a warm person.'

'And look where it got him,' Leo responded without skipping a beat. 'After my mother died, he couldn't cope with solitude so he allowed his emotions to carry him away and he ended up with Georgia. Need I say more?'

'He was vulnerable,' Sammy admitted, startled out of her idle gazing at his profile.

'He was vulnerable because he allowed himself to get swept away by his emotions. If that doesn't convince you that emotions are best left at the front door, think about Sean. I admit he was never the most focused guy in the world but who knows. He might have achieved something if he hadn't been taken in by Louise.'

'So your answer is to just…lock your emotions in a box and throw away the key?'

'It's stood me in excellent stead over the years.'

Sammy could now understand why his father was so desperate to have contact with Adele. He would have wanted to anyway because that was simply the kind of man he was, gentle and effusive and warm, but, with no prospect of his own son rushing down the aisle in a hurry to start the next generation of little Morgan-Whites, he probably saw Adele as his one and only chance of having what amounted to a grandchild.

'Don't you plan on marrying...for real?'

'Depends what you call *for real*,' Leo replied drily. 'If by *for real* you're asking whether I'll ever throw caution to the winds and nurture un-realistic expectations about fairy-tale romances lasting a lifetime, then no. Not a chance. If, on the other hand, you're asking whether I may one day seal a union with a woman with whom I can enjoy some intellectual banter, a woman who is financially self-sufficient in her own right and who has enough of a life of her own to not need constant attention, then who knows? It's a possibility, although it has to be said that it's nowhere near being on the horizon at this moment in time.'

'That sounds like a lot of fun,' Sammy couldn't resist saying and he burst out laugh-ing, a rich, sexy laugh that made her bloom with confusing, forbidden pleasure inside.

'Of course,' he murmured, 'there would also

have to be certain things in place for the equation to work.'

'Like what?'

He briefly took his eyes off the road to look at her and Sammy felt bright colour crawl up from the tips of her toes to her hairline because she realised immediately what those *certain things* were.

Flustered, she looked away and stared straight out through the window, out into an unlit blackness, and heard him burst out laughing again.

'So you see,' he murmured when his laughter had trailed off, 'this little rescue package is as much of a hardship for me as it is for you. Not only will my working habits have to be constrained but so will my—'

'I get it,' she interrupted hastily.

He laughed again and then asked conversationally, 'Not the same for you?'

'I don't change boyfriends,' Sammy retorted coldly, 'the way I change outfits.'

'Now, now, are you implying that I do?'

'Don't you?'

'I'm not looking for love ever after,' he told her. 'But I enjoy having fun and I enjoy being in the company of women who like having fun with me.'

'It's just as well this is a fake engagement,' Sammy told him airily, while her mind toyed feverishly with images of him *having fun with his fun women*.

'Because you're looking for your soulmate?'

'That's right. There's nothing wrong with that.' She thought of her ex-boyfriends and marvelled that the theory of the perfect soulmate could be so different from the reality. It didn't mean that the guy for her wasn't out there. It just meant that she had to kiss one or two frogs before she got to him.

'Well, to each their own.' Leo shrugged indifferently. 'And that, as I said before, is just one of the reasons why this is such a good fake engagement. We're not even beginning to sing from the same song sheet when it comes to relationships. Now, let's talk about how we met and how long we've been seeing one another.'

The sleet had turned to snow by the time they made it to Happenden Court, which crested a hill and was reached via a long tree-bordered avenue. In summer, it was a glorious approach to the magnificent country estate but now, in the bitter, biting wind, it was no less impressive but rather a bleak and haunting view, especially with nightfall fast approaching.

The house ahead, however, was bathed in light.

Sammy absolutely loved the house. Admittedly, it was way too big for one man on his own, but Harold had lived in a small group of rooms in the massive property, only opening up the rest of the house on special occasions. In summer, people actually paid to visit the gardens and the part of the historic house which was largely unused.

He claimed he couldn't part with it even though it was huge and expensive to maintain. Too many memories, he had told Sammy once.

'He needs to downsize.' Leo read her mind as he swung the car into the courtyard. 'He might be emotional, but he's as stubborn as a mule. Remember to look surprised when you walk through the door.'

'The entire village won't be there, will they? Hiding in the living room with the lights off?'

'That could be a dangerous approach to take, considering most of the assembled crowd are in their seventies and eighties. And remember to look as though you've found true love with me.'

'Why? Do you think they've got a hotline to the paparazzi?'

She knew how she sounded. Petulant and sulky and childish. And yes, she'd signed up for a deal with the devil and she knew that she should be taking it on the chin instead of moaning and groaning. And yes, he was right. Whether she liked to admit it or not, the financial pressures that had been keeping her awake for over a year would be erased. Like a teacher sweeping into the classroom, he would wipe the whiteboard clean and she would be able to start afresh.

How many times had she fantasised about this very thing?

But every time she looked at him, it hit home just how steep the price she would be paying was. He did something to her. He unsettled her. Between that and her conscience, the next few weeks were not going to be a walk in the park.

How could she pretend to be in love with someone who unsettled her? When she fundamentally disliked what he stood for? When his approach to life was so different from hers? Surely one glance and anyone would see through the sham. Especially Gail Jamieson, who had a lot to lose if she didn't gain custody of her granddaughter. They would be going to Australia and she would be playing out this charade in front of people who wouldn't be as forgiving and thrilled to see him engaged as the people waiting inside the house. Plus, deceiving people she had known since childhood didn't sit right and that, in itself, filled her with anxiety.

Thrilled they might be, but wouldn't they be able to see through her phoney smiles in a second? She could only hope that they would take their cue from her mother, who, after a long phone call with Sammy, knew the lie of the land.

'That's exactly what I'm talking about,' Leo grated, grinding the powerful car to a stop and turning to look at her as he killed the engine.

Sammy's thoughts were on her mother. She had been surprisingly upbeat about the situation, given the fact that it had been relayed by her daughter in a tone of voice that had been thick with resignation, doom and gloom.

But then her mother, Sammy reasoned, would have spent many more long hours as witness to Harold's despondency at not having his granddaughter in the same country. She would have lived through the nightmare of Gail's interference and demands and the horrible prospect of those demands continuing while any supportive role to Adele was shoved aside.

Plus she would have never argued that Sammy had made the wrong decision. If she *had* disagreed with her daughter, she would have kept her opinions to herself because the habit of being supportive of the decisions Sammy made was just too ingrained.

They had operated as a unit for a very long time.

'Sammy!'

'Huh?' Sammy blinked and surfaced out of her thoughts to focus on the man frowning at her.

Leo raked frustrated fingers through his hair and continued to frown at her because she'd been a million miles away just then. He'd been talking to her and, instead of paying attention to what he'd been saying, she'd blanked him out.

'I was *talking to you*,' he said grittily.

The surly edge to his voice suddenly lightened her mood and snapped her out of her thoughts. She looked at him, amused, because he had sounded, just then, like a sulky child.

'Care to share the joke?' He scowled and she grinned.

'You're angry because I wasn't giving you one hundred per cent of my attention? I guess,' she said shrewdly, 'you're not accustomed to women who don't give you *one hundred per cent* of their attention.'

'Don't be ridiculous,' Leo growled.

'I'm not! But just because you're *my fiancé*

doesn't mean that I have to agree with everything you say and snap to attention the second you give a command.'

'Rebelling and being argumentative isn't going to persuade anyone that we're an item. Now, out we go. They're waiting for us and don't forget to look shocked. There's nothing worse than someone who isn't suitably flabbergasted at a surprise party thrown for them.'

Almost at the door, she paused to rest her hand on his arm.

Leo looked down at her, expecting defiance and that mulish stubbornness he was fast becoming accustomed to. Instead, she looked suddenly vulnerable and defensive.

Her complexion was so satiny smooth that he found himself staring. She had carved a niche for herself in the background and she had done that by deliberately making sure to downplay every single asset she had.

But the more he looked at her, the more appealing her attraction seemed to be.

He shook himself out of this strange line of thought, inserted his key into the lock and turned it, pushing open the front door and stepping back to allow her past him.

It had been several weeks since Sammy had visited the house but, as always, she stood for a few minutes breathing in its spectacular, unique magnificence.

Despite the historic interest of the building, it still managed to look lived-in, probably because of the eclectic mix of period furniture and the scattering of beautiful objects which Leo's parents had gathered over the years.

Mariela, having come from some wealth herself, had brought with her paintings and art pieces that were wonderfully exotic and there were unique touches everywhere that gave the house a very special feel. On the highly polished circular table in the hallway there was a massive arrangement of fresh flowers and Sammy breathed in the wonderful floral scent, as powerful as incense, temporarily forgetting why she was here.

Blissful oblivion didn't last long. She heard the babble of voices from behind one of the doors and quailed.

'Chin up,' Leo commanded. 'We're in love. Don't look as though you have a hot date with the hangman.'

He was walking briskly towards the sitting room and she hustled in his wake, horribly self-conscious and frantically wondering how she was going to pull this all off whilst looking suitably surprised. And, of course, delighted.

She hoped that she might discover award-winning talents she had hitherto never suspected.

Leo knocked on the sitting room door then pushed it open and stood aside and, as she took a deep breath and hesitated, he pulled her into him and swung her round to face him.

He was smiling.

For a second, everything flew out of her head. This was a smile meant for her and, as she looked at him, she felt the whole room in front of her disappear—the voices, the people, the clinking of glasses, the laughter.

Her breath caught. Could she have forgotten how to breathe? Was that possible?

Her body was burning, her breasts aching and a strange sensation pooling between her thighs.

'Darling—' Leo laughed '—a little surprise party for us. I wanted to tell you but I was sworn to secrecy...'

This in a voice just loud enough to generate a round of delighted applause from, as she'd feared, at least forty of the great and the good from the village, all people she had known since forever.

And now she was going to have to look rapturous.

She began to turn and then he caught her face in his hands and lowered his head...

And kissed her. The tip of his tongue teased her full lower lip and Sammy instinctively opened her mouth, her whole body leaning into him, wanting the feel of his hard masculine body against hers. The taste of his tongue against hers sent desire ripping through her with the force of a raging inferno.

She didn't understand her powerful, immediate response to his caress. She just knew that it owned her.

And then he drew back, leaving her trembling and dazed, mouth swollen from his kiss, eyes over-bright and glittering.

'Excellent,' he murmured into her ear. 'I think it's safe to say that you don't have to worry about stage fright any more. We couldn't have been more convincing.'

CHAPTER FOUR

THE WHOLE VILLAGE now knew that Harold Morgan-White's son was engaged to lovely little Sammy Wilson. And wasn't it just fantastic because hadn't Harold been complaining for *years* about his overworked, stressed out son who was never going to settle down?

'If we don't escape soon,' he had told her as the last of the guests was being shown to the door, 'the next surprise occasion will include the vicar, the organist and a marriage service.'

'Our parents would never allow that,' Sammy had been quick to refute. 'Not when they know that this isn't for real.' But you wouldn't have guessed it from the way his father and her mother had basked in the congratulatory attention.

And she knew that to outside eyes she would have appeared equally thrilled because she had spent the remainder of the evening with that kiss still burning her lips. He had caught her off guard and had done the one thing which he must have known would have brought hectic colour to her cheeks and left her speechless.

It turned out she had had award-winning skills of deception in spades.

Lest she forget that they were a couple in love, he had made sure to stick close to her side for the duration of the party. His hand had lain possessively around her waist and she marvelled that no one sought to question this sudden, overwhelming love affair that had smothered the pair of them.

Whatever happened to common sense?

And, whilst she could acknowledge that Leo was a good-looking, sophisticated and very sexy man, how was it that she could have cast aside all her doubts and allowed herself to be so affected by a kiss that had been purely for the benefit of the assembled crowd?

Since then, she had not seen him. He had returned to London to work on deals he needed to close before they left for Australia and she had used the time to hand in her notice, much to the disappointment of the head teacher.

And now, as she stared at the suitcases on the floor in her bedroom in her mother's house, she felt as though she had stepped onto a roller coaster that was picking up speed. It had nudged slowly to the top and she was poised, looking down at the loops stretching ahead of her.

She couldn't stop gazing at the costly engagement ring on her finger and vaguely wondering how she had ended up where she had, all in the space of a week.

But then she knew, didn't she…?

Leo had appealed to the very powerful part of her that had wanted to see her mother's stress alleviated, the part of her that had been frantically worrying about money, about the bank, about how much debt had piled up over the months. The part of her that had been worrying about her future and where she wanted to go with it.

Into this Leo had charged, with heady solutions and a price to pay…because there was no such thing as a free lunch.

Had she not, reluctantly, felt sympathy for his cause she would have turned her back on his offer, but she was deeply fond of his father and had easily been able to see how the end could justify the means, even though deception was something she found abhorrent. She had also heard enough about Gail Jamieson and about Sean and his constant leeching of his ex-stepfather's bank account to know that Adele would not have a glorious, warm and loving environment if she stayed with her grandmother, who was, from all accounts, even more grasping than her daughter and son-in-law had been.

But, in return, she had had a glimpse of how difficult it was going to be to play the part of loving fiancée because being with Leo was just so unsettling.

She wasn't cool enough to deal with his massive presence. She had never liked the way he treated women and she disapproved of his casual approach to relationships and while neither of these things should have mattered because she and he were only linked by virtue of the charade they were playing, they somehow did.

She heard her mother calling her, carolling that the driver had arrived, courtesy of Leo, who had firmly decreed that a train to the airport wasn't going to do.

She lugged the cases down and found her mother waiting at the bottom of the stairs.

'Are you sure you're going to be all right while I'm gone?' Sammy asked worriedly. 'It will only be for ten days, by which time Leo should have a clear idea of what the outcome of the custody battle is going to be.'

Her mother's thin face was as bright-eyed as

Sammy had seen it in a very long time. Which, frankly, was also worrying. She hoped her mother wasn't going to start believing that the pretence was for real. However, this was hardly the time to angst over that when the chauffeur was waiting.

'I'll be absolutely fine, darling. Amy is going to pop over every morning and I don't have any hospital appointments until you're back anyway. You just go out there and, well, enjoy yourself. It's been such a long time since you've had a break.'

'Mum,' Sammy whispered sotto voce as the chauffeur entered and, after a brief cheery smile, headed to the car with her cases. 'This isn't going to be about *having a break*. Remember I told you when I… Well, when I told you what this is all about?'

Her mother's eyes rounded and she smiled reassuringly, 'Of course and you're doing the right thing, darling. Harold is so relieved that this whole business is going to be sorted out once and for all.'

'Well, no one knows what the outcome is going to be,' Sammy pointed out constrainedly.

'It'll be fine with Leo in charge.'

Sammy rolled her eyes, halfway out of the

door. 'He's not a knight in shining armour—he can't conquer everything!'

'Harold has a lot of faith in him and, by the way, Sam, you look lovely.'

'Mum, I have to go.' Her face was red. So what if Leo had breezily insinuated that her wardrobe only needed minor tweaks and packages full of beautiful, understated pieces that fitted her perfectly had subsequently arrived at her front door. If he had complained and tried to force her into wearing anything she hadn't wanted to wear then she would have dug her heels in and stood her ground, but he hadn't.

As the car ate up the miles between Salcombe and London, she wondered what he would think when she removed her coat and cardigan to reveal her lightweight cream trousers and her tan tee shirt and when she stashed away her boots, essential against the snow which had been falling when she'd left Devon, and pulled out her cream loafers. She was all covered up in her thick waterproof coat and scarf and gloves, but underneath was evidence of the effort she was making to fit the part.

Of course there would be no male appreciation in his eyes; as he had made clear from the very start, she was the ideal candidate because there would be no temptation for him to come near her. Unless circumstances dictated and he had to for show.

Or, at any rate, something like that.

She was a paid employee and, if it weren't for this weird situation, he certainly wouldn't be seeking her out to spend time in her company.

They made excellent progress and her nerves fluttered as she was helped out of the car with her bags and then, by some prior arrangement only possible, she assumed, with very, very rich and influential people, the chauffeur was permitted to leave his car outside the airport so that she could be delivered to the check-in desk without the hassle of having to manage a trolley herself.

Sammy had never experienced anything like it and although she didn't want to be impressed, she really was.

The crowd parted. People stared and whispered. Someone took a picture. Sammy felt like royalty. She wished she had had the foresight to dump the untrendy coat and scarf before exiting the car.

Cheeks burning, she was relieved to find Leo waiting for her by the first-class check-in desk.

He watched her slow progress towards him. Her hair was loose and it curled and danced around her heart-shaped face, falling in unrestrained ringlets past her shoulders. It was every shade of blond—vanilla streaked with gold with hints of strawberry—and it was brilliantly eye-catching.

The turquoise clarity of her eyes, fringed with dark, dark lashes which were at odds with her blond, blond hair also made him want to stare, he thought distractedly as she abruptly came to a halt in front of him.

'You're here,' he said, lounging indolently against the counter while his driver dealt with the business of the bags on the belt.

'Did you think I wouldn't turn up?'

'Your attitude when we last parted company wasn't reassuring.'

Sammy blushed. She could breathe him in and it was like breathing in some kind of dangerous, mind-altering drug. She stepped back a little.

'I'm glad to see you're wearing the engagement ring.' He took her hand in his and inspected her finger, looking at it from several angles while she fought the temptation to snatch it away.

'I put it on in the car,' she confessed, once she had her burning hand back to herself. 'I didn't want to wear it in front of my mum.' They had checked in and were moving with purpose through the airport, away from the crowds and the duty-free shops and directly towards the first-class lounge. Sammy followed in a daze, eyes darting around her, feeling that sneaky, pleasurable important feeling again because she knew that people were staring sideways at them. He commanded so much attention without even realising it because he looked neither left nor right and was uninterested in everyone around them.

'Why not?'

'She knows that this is just a…a…*charade*, but…'

'But what?'

'I just don't want her to get it into her head that there's any part of this that might actually be for real.'

'No.' Leo looked sideways at her. 'I'm sure she won't.'

'Yes, well, you can never tell,' Sammy continued, pausing only to stare around her at the lounge into which he had led her. It was beyond luxurious, the sort of place where you just knew that nearly everyone was stupidly rich and probably famous. 'Wow,' she couldn't help whispering as they came to a clutch of sofas.

'Wow?' Leo raised his eyebrows, amused at her lack of artifice. She was feisty, outspoken, stubborn as the proverbial mule and would certainly prove to be a challenging assault on his well-ordered world over the next ten days, but no one could accuse her of being anything but glaringly honest in her responses.

'I've never travelled like this in my life before,' Sammy said truthfully. 'In fact, I've only been on a plane twice in my entire life and it was nothing like this.'

'You can take your coat off and sit down.' Leo never paid a scrap of attention to the luxury that surrounded him wherever he went. Now, he glanced around him at the subdued, well-bred, quiet lounge that screamed *exclusivity*. Right about now, any of the women he was accustomed to dating would have stripped off her coat and would have been indulging in the sport of twisting and twirling and making sure that all eyes in the room were focused on her. Sammy was still in her coat. It looked as though she might actually have pulled it more tightly around her.

'You were telling me about your mother getting the wrong idea...' He began removing his laptop from his leather case, absently glancing at the headlines of the newspaper neatly folded on the table in front of the chairs.

He looked up.

The coat was off, as was the scarf. She was bending slightly to unzip her boots.

When he looked at her he could clearly see the outline of her breasts as she leant down. Her tee shirt was figure-hugging, the lightweight trousers lovingly contoured every rounded inch of her bottom and the surprising length of her slim legs. She wasn't looking at him. She was busy shoving the unsightly boots into a bag she had brought with her, replacing them with some cream shoes that complemented the outfit.

Nothing was revealing. There was nothing at all remotely attention-grabbing about what she was wearing. Yet she still managed to grab his attention and hold on to it.

Shoes on and outer layers removed and neatly folded and shoved into her carry-on, aside from the boots, which she had crammed into a canvas bag brought specially for that purpose, Sammy straightened and met his eyes.

For a few seconds she held her breath and wondered whether he would say anything about her outfit. When he didn't, the disappointment felt disproportionate but she pinned a smile on her face anyway.

She brutally reminded herself that there was nothing between them so there was no reason for him to remark on anything she chose to wear. As long as she played her part and gave no one any reason to suspect that there was anything amiss between them, especially when they reached their destination, then conversation would remain perfunctory.

'Yes—' she sat down and tucked her hair behind her ears '—I think that Mum's a little vulnerable because she's been ill. She's always been a strong woman and to have to accept that she wasn't as strong as she thought she was hit her hard.' Sammy frowned. 'It's only recently occurred to me, from a couple of things that Mum's said, that she was worried sick about leaving me single.' She laughed a little self-consciously. 'She seemed to think that if anything happened to her, I might have needed the support of someone by my side.'

'And you think that that worry might lead her to pin her hopes on this becoming more than just a fake engagement?' Leo was trying hard to quell his surging libido, which had suddenly decided to put in an appearance. He wondered why she dressed to hide her body when she had the sort of body that most men would drool over. Unashamedly *feminine* and sexy in its femininity.

'She actually told me that I should enjoy myself in Melbourne because I hadn't had a break in a long time,' Sammy confided.

'And there's no chance of that happening?'

Sammy opened her mouth to ask him how on earth she could possibly relax when she was going to be spending her time there in his company, pretending to be his fiancée.

But she stopped.

Why wouldn't she be able to relax? He would. He would work and when he wasn't working he certainly wouldn't be stressing out because his nerves were all over the place when he was in her company. His stomach wouldn't be doing somersaults when he was in her radius.

'I've spent so long worrying over stuff that I've forgotten how to relax,' she said vaguely, thinking on her feet.

'Then I'll have to change that.'

'What do you mean?'

'Engaged people go places, explore, seek out exciting new adventures.'

'Are you joking?'

'Why would I be joking, Sammy? We have to be convincing and if we spend our free time on opposite sides of the city it won't be long before Jamieson smells a rat.'

'But she's not going to be following us everywhere, is she?'

'Quite frankly,' Leo said with genuine honesty, 'I wouldn't put it past the woman. Think about it. If she loses custody of Adele, she loses access to my money. I owe her nothing. She's not related to me or to my father in any way whatsoever. As long as she can hang on to the child, she is guaranteed an income because neither my father nor, frankly, myself, would want Adele to suffer financial hardship. The tie with my father may not be secured with blood but it's there. So, that being the case, she'll do anything in her power to discredit me and what's the fastest way of discrediting me? By convincing a judge that I'm not the reliable, happily soon-to-be married man I claim to be.'

'I suppose so.'

'So you'll get the break your mother wants you to have,' he told her with silky assurance. 'Now—' he indicated the long counter brimming with delicious snacks '—why don't you go and help yourself? If I'm to have to focus on the custody battle while maintaining our happily engaged façade by mixing in some fun in the sun for the next week and a half, I might as well do as much work as I can while I'm still here.'

Despite what Leo had said about making sure that they stuck to their brief as the loved-up engaged couple, Sammy privately didn't think that anyone in Melbourne would give a hoot whether they looked loved-up or not. And whilst she had heard all sorts of rumours about Gail and her horrendous ways, she honestly couldn't picture the woman creeping around behind them wherever they went, in disguise, with the specific aim of trying to prove them liars.

Exhausted after twenty-two hours of flying, she was dazed as she emerged from the plane. He'd bought every seat in the first-class cabin because sharing space wasn't his 'thing' and it was less hassle than organising his company Gulfstream—and, besides, arriving in full view on a chartered airline worked. It was jaw-dropping extravagance but she had soon discovered that being up in the air for hours and hours and hours on end took its toll, however luxurious the seating arrangements.

Accustomed to functioning wherever he happened to be, and adept at working in the confines of a plane, Leo had not been disconcerted at all. He had pulled out his computer and had spent the majority of the flight working.

At some point, with neither her book or the range of movies netting her attention, she had turned to him and said airily, 'Do you ever get bored?'

'When it comes to work—' he had turned the full wattage of his attention onto her and she had felt, suddenly and inexplicably, like a flower, wilting in the shadows, exposed to the full force of the sun's rays '—I have an inexhaustible supply of energy. I also have to wrap up some pretty important deals before we reach Melbourne. Like I said, fun in the sun is the equivalent of taking time out and taking time out isn't something I can afford to do.'

'When was the last time you had a holiday?'

'You're beginning to sound like my father,' Leo had said wryly. 'Please do me a favour and spare me the long lectures about high blood pressure, premature heart attacks and stress.'

'I wasn't going to start lecturing you about anything,' Sammy had informed him. 'I was just curious and you don't have to think that you have to spend all your spare time with me. In fact, does Ms Jamieson even know exactly when we're due over?'

'You can't imagine that I would make this trip on the off-chance of finding her, do you? I have meetings arranged in advance with her lawyer and I have a team of people at my end, waiting and ready to go. I've made very sure to cage her in. Wouldn't want her to consider bolting.'

For a brief moment, Sammy had almost felt sorry for the woman. She had certainly understood in that moment why his father had had such an unshakeable faith in him securing the outcome that was desired.

He exuded absolute mastery.

But she had still privately thought that, whilst it sometimes paid to be cautious, he was being overcautious when it came to maintaining their charade.

Blistering heat greeted them as they emerged into the soaring summer temperatures. The sky was flamboyantly blue and cloudless and the strength of the heat was formidable. In her tee shirt and slacks, which she had traded on the plane for a set of silk pyjamas, she still felt her skin begin to perspire almost immediately.

She knew that they would be met by a chauffeur. She hadn't known that, along with the chauffeur who was dutifully waiting for them, there would also be a little cluster of paparazzi.

Startled and blinking, she instinctively stepped closer to Leo and felt his arm curve around her as he led her directly to the car waiting for them.

Once inside the air-conditioned space, Sammy craned back, staring at the reporters, then turned to Leo and whispered urgently, 'What on earth were they doing at the airport? I don't get it. We didn't have any of this in England. In fact, other than the people at the party, no one even knows that we're engaged!'

'What gives you that idea?'

'Why would anyone know? There certainly wasn't anyone taking pictures…'

'I've made sure to keep it low-key,' Leo informed her and she looked at him in utter astonishment.

'What do you mean?'

He was sprawled in the seat, leaning against the door, his big body angled to face her. Dressed in grey trousers and a short-sleeved black polo shirt with a tiny discreet insignia embroidered on one side, he was the last word in sophistication. He had *that look*. The look of someone who should be photographed. Rich. Powerful. Influential.

She recalled the way his mouth had felt against hers and quivered.

'I have an excellent relationship with the press, particularly the tabloid press. They're like sharks. They'll cheerfully rip you apart if it takes their fancy. It's always a good idea to keep them onside. I'm wealthy, I'm powerful but I'm not a Hollywood star. The less they print about me, the better, but I accept that my movements are sometimes of interest.' He shrugged. Sammy found it fascinating that he could sit there and talk about a world that was so foreign to her. He really and truly moved in a completely different hemisphere. A world where people were photographed and simple day-to-day things became newsworthy events to be recorded for public consumption.

No wonder he had reasoned that her presence by his side would give his cause gravitas. She was the embodiment of everything that was contrary to all of that—the embodiment of *normality*—just the sort of reassuring thing the lawyers would make note of when it came to sorting out custody of an impressionable young child.

Guilt shook her because this *normality* was only going to last as long as it took for him to have Adele under his wing.

She consoled herself with the thought that whatever was brought to the table by Leo and his wonderful, kind-hearted father was sure to be better than what lay in store for the little girl at the hands of a grasping grandmother, but she still backed away from thinking too hard about the rights and wrongs.

At the end of the day, she thought uneasily, it wasn't her problem.

Besides, whilst the world of extreme wealth was not one she inhabited, she knew that there were very many children of wealthy parents who did very well on a diet of private schools and boarding schools and nannies.

'I know a couple of the reporters,' Leo said as though it were the most normal thing in the world. 'The trick is to see them as humans in their own right and not a collection of pests. Humanise them and they're more likely to humanise *you* in return. At any rate, I spread the word that I was engaged and made it known that a flashy announcement wasn't going to do. I felt that was appropriate, given the circumstances, but no point broadcasting it when it's going to come to an end in due course.'

'No, quite.' She was finding it hard to keep up.

'They listened and did as I asked.'

'People do that, don't they?' she murmured and he looked at her and nodded.

'Different story over here,' Leo informed her. 'Ignore anyone who asks for an interview. I may not be as well known as I am in London but I do have considerable financial interests in this part of the world and...' He flushed darkly and paused, and something about that pause roused her curiosity.

'And what?'

'I did achieve a certain amount of unwanted notoriety for dating a certain Australian actress about a year ago.'

'Really?' Sammy had been so wrapped up in concerns about her mother's health at that time that she doubted she would have been able to remember anything that had been going on around her, never mind what had been unravelling in the gossip pages of tabloid newspapers.

'Vivienne Madison.'

'*The* Vivienne Madison? Gosh. I had no idea. What happened?'

'I'm surprised you missed out that little slice of my life,' Leo inserted wryly, 'considering you seem to have spotted me in the centre pages of tabloids in the past.'

'I wasn't really with it a year ago,' Sammy admitted. 'Mum was undergoing treatment and I was…in a different place. A scary place. I was barely functioning. I mean, I was going to work but taking a lot of time off and I couldn't focus at all. I don't think I glanced at a newspaper once for months.'

'The long and short of it,' Leo said heavily, 'was that she was found with a bottle of pills in a hotel room and the baying Australian press decided to go for me.'

'You mean she tried to commit suicide because you left her?' Immediately, she could feel herself pull back from him, deeply appalled that his way of life, his cavalier attitude towards women, might have resulted in someone actually attempting to take her own life as a result of being ditched.

Leo read the distaste on her face. Normally, this would not have fazed him. He never saw the need to launch into explanations for his behaviour or to justify decisions he had taken. As long as he stuck to his impeccable moral code and recognised his own personal truths, who gave a damn what other people thought?

But, for some reason, he didn't like the thoughts he knew were churning around in her head.

'Vivienne Madison was a seriously unstable woman.' He was unfamiliar with the process of explaining himself and found that his words did not come as easily as usual. 'When I became involved with her, I discovered that she had a drinking problem. She was also, I later found out, hooked on painkillers. But she was an amazing actress and managed to hide both those dependencies.' He sighed, his lean, handsome face unusually empathetic, the cold lines temporarily erased. 'She became dependent on me very quickly, although I had told her from the very beginning that I was not interested in settling down. But she was a highly emotional person and her addictions made her even more irrational than she otherwise might have been. I knew that it had to end but I made sure to get her signed up with an excellent counsellor as well as a rehab centre noted for its success rate. I may not have wanted her in my life but I wasn't going to cast her aside like a pile of used rubbish. The truth is that I felt deeply sorry for her.'

Sammy was impressed. That this formidable and ruthlessly controlled man was capable of compassion for a woman he had no longer wanted in his life was an eye-opener.

It didn't *mean* anything, but it certainly afforded her a different take on him. It was peculiarly complimentary to him because she could tell that he was less than comfortable telling this story and was doubtless only doing so in case it came out and she knew nothing about it. As his fiancée, it would be surprising if she was ignorant of what had happened.

'The incident with the overdose was several weeks after we had parted company but that was something the press over here omitted to mention. Later, there was a nondescript apology to me when they discovered that the overdose was in response to a rejection from one of the psychiatrists at the rehab centre. At any rate, my name will be linked to hers forever over here.'

'And is she still in contact with you?'

'In no way, shape or form,' Leo asserted.

That was the end of the conversation. She could see that on his face but it left her thinking that she could almost understand his antipathy towards emotional situations. He had had a substantial amount of experience in dealing with the negative side of them.

'So we have a schedule here,' she said, changing the subject.

'Meetings lined up with lawyers. I expect some sort of compensation will have to be given to Ms Jamieson if custody is awarded to me. It will be a very busy ten days.'

'Not much time for fun in the sun.'

'Tut-tut,' Leo said lazily. 'Is that the right approach for a newly engaged woman to be taking? I'm sure we'll find the time to escape and see some of Melbourne's sights, especially if there are interested parties pursuing us who need to be placated. Like nosy journalists. If Jamieson is playing hardball, then there's every chance she's got in touch with a newspaper and filled them in on what I'm doing over here. It's certainly got the ingredients for a good story, especially with my past association with Vivienne. But don't worry—' he reached out and slid his long brown finger along her arm, sending splinters of awareness skittering through her like quicksilver '—it'll be over in no time at all and you can return to your life.'

CHAPTER FIVE

IT DIDN'T TAKE long before the car was pulling up outside a grand hotel and they stepped back out into the searing heat. It felt strange to be in a busy, vibrant city and yet to know that the sea was just a hop and a skip away. Sammy imagined that she could almost smell the salt in the air.

And the people looked different. Relaxed, sun-kissed, moving at a slower pace. She had to keep reminding herself that this wasn't the break her mother had told her she needed but she could still feel a holiday spirit pushing through until they were shown up to their massive suite and she gazed around in confusion because there was just the one bedroom.

'Is this it?' she asked, as soon as their bags were deposited and the bellboy had left, quietly closing the door behind him.

Leo, immune to his surroundings as always, was heading to the well-stocked kitchen where he proceeded to fetch them both a bottle of ice-cold water. 'You'll find yourself drinking this by the gallon,' he promised. 'I would recommend that you carry a bottle in your bag whenever you're out. The heat over here can be ferocious and we don't want you getting dehydrated, do we?'

Sammy took the bottle from him. 'Thank you very much for your health tips, Leo, but where is *my* bedroom?'

Leo carried on drinking, looking at her as he drank, then, dumping the empty bottle on the kitchen counter and strolling towards the sitting area, he nodded in the direction of the bedroom.

'What?' She tripped along and watched as he coolly pulled out his computer and flipped it open, attention focused on whatever he had called up to peruse.

'Leo, could you at least look at me when I'm trying to have a conversation?'

'You wanted to know where your bedroom is and I showed you. It's behind me and yes, there's only the one room.'

'But…'

'But what did you expect, Sammy?'

'Not just one bedroom with one bed in it!'

'No?' he drawled coolly. 'Did you think that

I would book us into separate rooms? Maybe on different floors? Or why stop there? Different hotels?'

'You're deliberately misunderstanding me.'

'I'm not deliberately misunderstanding you. Frankly, I think you are the one deliberately misunderstanding the situation. Did you honestly imagine that as a newly engaged couple we wouldn't be sharing a bedroom?'

'I hadn't thought about it,' Sammy stuttered.

'Engaged couples tend to share bedrooms these days. There was no chance, after all of this, that I would risk anyone suspecting that all is not what it appears to be in the land of the soon-to-be wed lovebirds.'

He was right, of course. They weren't living in an era of chaperoned walks in the park and a ban on all forms of physical contact bar holding hands.

She hadn't really thought about that angle at all, just as she hadn't really thought about how open to scrutiny they would be because she had had no idea of the world he occupied.

Sammy dropped into the chair facing him. She wondered how she hadn't really noticed the huge differences between them sooner and then thought that that was probably because she hadn't seen him on enough of a regular basis over the years and, when she *had* seen him, it had always been in the rural setting of his father's house. She had ceased to be awestruck at the mansion in which Harold lived and he was such a lovable and down-to-earth man that, in the setting of his rolling country estate, Leo had been a lot more of an ordinary guy.

But he *wasn't* an ordinary guy. This *wasn't* going to be a low-key two-week situation. He *hadn't* overplayed the amount of attention they might generate.

'We're in this together for the next week and a half, so you might as well get used to it.'

'Thank goodness it's just going to be for a week and a half,' Sammy breathed with sincerity. 'I don't think I could live in it for any longer than that.'

'Oh, really?'

Leo imbued those two simple words with such sarcastic disbelief that she flushed and glared at him.

'I wouldn't want to live in a goldfish bowl,' she asserted dismissively. 'I'd hate to think that there might be people with cameras wherever I went, waiting to get a picture of me.'

'And yet you seemed to be mightily impressed by the first-class lounge and the first-class cabin and the chauffeur-driven car...'

Sammy blushed, hating him just at that moment because he was right; she really *had* enjoyed that feeling of being treated like royalty.

'That's because it's a novelty. I'd soon tire of it,' she insisted and he shrugged with an expression that indicated that he was suddenly bored with the whole conversation.

'Which is just as well,' Leo drawled, 'considering the novelty isn't going to last very long. It would be a nuisance if you started getting too accustomed to it.'

'Meaning?'

'Like I said to you before, you're ideal for this role because you wouldn't be interested in prolonging it. Indeed, the fact that you don't like this lifestyle could come in very handy when it comes to citing reasons for our break-up. Two people, opposites drawn together by a powerful attraction only, sadly, to discover that opposites, in the end, do not have what it takes to make lasting relationships. But, getting back to the matter of the bedroom… We're sharing it and I'm afraid you're just going to have to deal with that. Let's not forget here that you're not in this because you're an altruistic saint only concerned with my father's welfare. You're in this because the price was right.'

Sammy went bright red. He had sliced

through the waffle and got straight to the point and she couldn't dispute the truth of what he was saying.

She also knew that, for what she was being paid, sharing a bedroom was not exactly too high a price to pay. And what, exactly, was her cause for concern, anyway? It wasn't as though he was attracted to her. In fact, she could tell that he was struggling not to let his attention wander back to whatever report she had interrupted. And as soon as they were away from public view, he made no attempt to come near her or to even look at her as though she belonged to the female sex.

She was only his type when she had to be, which was when they were being observed.

She stood up stiffly. 'Okay. Fair enough.'

Leo's dark-eyed gaze narrowed. So she had bought into a situation and was now discovering that it came with certain clauses she might not have taken into account. He felt a degree of sympathy for her, even though he had no intention of revealing that because, as far as he was concerned, when you put your signature on the dotted line you agreed to all the terms and conditions.

But she wasn't like the women he was accustomed to dating. Naturally, she would have had experience of sharing a bed with a man—she wasn't a teenager, after all—but he was a virtual stranger and she was weirdly disingenuous.

Yet, after her initial appalled reaction, she had accepted it without further ado.

'You're perfectly safe with me,' he told her roughly and Sammy paused, her heartbeat suddenly accelerating as their eyes met.

She didn't know what to say and even if there had been anything remotely resembling a coherent thought in her head she wouldn't have been able to vocalise it because her mouth was dry and her vocal cords had stopped working.

'You don't have to worry,' he explained into the deafening silence, 'that I'm going to lunge for you in the middle of the night. I would offer to sleep on the sofa but it seems a ridiculous amount of hassle to make a sofa up with whatever spare linen we can rustle up from a cupboard, only to *unmake* it first thing in the morning.'

'I'm not complaining.' Sammy finally found her voice and was pleased that it sounded relatively normal. 'I was just a little taken aback, that's all.' She told herself that this was a job, as he had made sure to remind her, and part of the job would be to sleep next to him. No big deal. She would be well and truly covered up. It wasn't as though her change of wardrobe had extended to a collection of French knickers and frilly negligees. It would be as unthreatening as if she were sleeping next to a potted plant.

'If you don't mind, I think I'll go have a bath now, freshen up. What are our plans for tomorrow?' She was still furiously trying to quieten her nerves at the prospect of sharing a bed with him and pretending that he was the equivalent of a potted plant.

Leo afforded her his sole undivided attention for a few seconds. 'I expect,' he said slowly, 'that it will involve you meeting the Jamieson woman at some point. My lawyers have emailed me over the proposal they've put to her lawyers and instinct tells me that she's not going to be over the moon. That's in the afternoon. Tomorrow morning, I suggest we visit a few shops.'

'Why?'

'Is that your response to the offer of going shopping?' Leo was amused.

'I don't like shopping,' Sammy admitted. She tilted her chin at a defiant angle. 'You can probably see for yourself why!'

'Come again?'

Sammy spread her hands down in a sweeping

gesture and laughed. 'I'm not exactly built like a model. You, of all people, should be able to see that for yourself, considering you only date models. And actresses who have model bodies.'

'What does that have to do with anything?' Leo was genuinely bewildered and Sammy was already regretting her impulse to put herself down but, when it came to her appearance, it was something that had always come as second nature. If you laughed at yourself first, then it deflected other people from laughing at you.

'When you have a figure like mine, twirling in front of mirrors in changing rooms is a bit of an ordeal,' she said lightly, scuttling in small steps towards the bedroom door. 'You probably wouldn't understand,' she embellished, more embarrassed by the second.

'And that would be because…?'

'You must know that you're a good-looking guy!' She wondered how the conversation had strayed so quickly from her simple enquiry as to what the plans were for the following day. 'I don't suppose mirrors pose a problem for you. Anyway—' she brushed aside the conversation, uncomfortable under his perceptive gaze '—you were talking about shopping. Why are we going shopping? There are loads of other things I'd rather be doing.'

'I'm in complete agreement with you there. However, you're going out with me now, we're engaged and it would seem odd for you to be seen wearing cheap off-the-peg clothes.'

Sammy's mouth dropped open. 'You said you weren't interested in telling me what I could or couldn't wear.'

'And I'm not, although I confess that I'm relieved you took the decision yourself to put the jeans and baggy tops on the back burner while we're out here.'

'So if you don't care what I wear, then what's the shopping expedition all about?' she bristled, fired up at an implied insult behind the suggestion. 'I'll bet you've never hinted to any of those women you've been out with in the past that you wanted to take them shopping because you didn't like their choice of clothing!'

'That's a thought,' Leo murmured, remembering what she had said about not liking shopping experiences. He didn't get why she would feel self-conscious of her body because there was an earthy voluptuousness about her that was powerfully attractive.

His eyes wandered.

She had slender legs, and a waist that was a handspan slim, but her breasts were generous and her hips were downright sinful in their curves, fashioned to be contoured by a man's hands.

He looked away, frowning at his brief loss of self-control.

'Maybe—' he thought of his exes and their minimalist approach to clothing '—I should have steered some of my past girlfriends to items of dress that weren't the size of paper tissues. A diet of relentlessly non-existent clothing can get very boring for a guy after a while.'

'You don't mean that.' But she was foolishly touched that he had made an effort to counteract any offence she might have taken by indulging in a little white lie.

'It's not about *what* you choose to wear. It's about the *quality* of what you choose to wear.'

'I can't afford to blow my savings on clothes,' Sammy told him abruptly.

'You probably could,' Leo countered with cool, restrained honesty, 'when this little charade is over. But that's by the by. What I'm saying is that any woman of mine would be expected to be wearing the very best. The very best in twinsets and pearls, if that happened to be her choice.'

Sammy stared at him and then she burst out laughing. 'You have got to be kidding!'

Leo frowned. 'Why would I be kidding?'

'Leo, I'm not the kind of girl who expects any man to buy her clothes for her! That's incredibly old-fashioned.'

'And what sort of girl would you be describing?' he enquired with the sort of shuttered expression that would have signalled a warning to her across the bows had she not still been smirking at the concept of a man paying for what she wore.

'Oh, just an airhead who traipses along from shop to shop, happy for you to dip into your wallet to fund her wardrobe.'

'Have you ever,' he asked, 'been treated to a shopping spree by one of these chauvinistic dinosaur guys you don't approve of?'

'Well…'

'So that's a *no*. Maybe you should give it a try before you start passing judgement. The fact of the matter is this, as my fiancée, you would be treated like a queen. There's no way I would countenance you going out in cheap supermarket bulk-buy clothes. You would wear the very best, in whatever you chose to wear.'

'I didn't get my outfits in a supermarket.'

'You know where I'm going with this, Sammy. Were this real, I would want you to be wearing the very best. It would give me pleasure to indulge you.'

Sammy went bright red. The deep, sexy timbre of his voice conjured up an image of this big, powerful man entranced enough with a woman to be possessive, generous and proud.

'But it isn't real.' She headed straight back down to earth before wayward images in her head could start giving her a thrill that would have been utterly inappropriate.

'No,' Leo agreed smoothly, 'it isn't. But, since that's not the image we're aiming to project, you're just going to have to subject yourself to the torture of the shopping trip.' He raised his eyebrows and looked at her speculatively. 'Who knows...maybe you'll enjoy it more than you expect. And if at the end of this you're too proud to keep the clothes you've bought you can always hand them back to me. A charity shop would be more than happy to take the discards.'

Sammy couldn't dwell on any of that for long because she was wandering back off to the appalling prospect of sharing a bed with him. Somehow she had convinced herself to forget about that while they had been sparring but her apprehension swamped her all over again as she locked herself in the bathroom and took her time having the longest bath in living memory, while listening out to hear whether he had entered the bedroom.

Her very-respectable pyjamas were neatly folded on the little circular table in the enormous bathroom. She only wished she weren't so nervous because her nerves prevented her from enjoying what had to be the most luxurious bathing experience of her life. The bathroom was a vision of pale marble, oversized fluffy towels, a walk-in wet room and a bath big enough to stage a concert.

Just like that, she thought back to him asking her whether she had ever been treated to a shopping spree by a guy. She was very quick to condemn the thought of it, and she knew that she wasn't going to *have fun* choosing clothes which someone she barely knew was going to feel obliged to pay for, but, that said, here she was, enjoying the splendour of a hotel he was paying for.

What did that say? She had always prided herself on her ability to stand on her own two feet. From an early age, she and her mother had presented a united front, soldiering on after her father's premature death. She had learned how to carry the weight of responsibility on her shoulders and that had been truly put to the test when her mother had fallen ill.

She had also learned not to depend on something as frivolous as her looks to get her through and, yes, she had privately nurtured some scorn for those women who relied on their appearance to provide the rungs on the ladder they could use to clamber upwards.

She wasn't going to turn to crafty feminine traits to see her through!

But something about Leo made her feel feminine. She found herself responding to his blatant masculinity in ways that were girlish and light-headed. She had wanted him to compliment her on her choice of dress and she could only blame the bizarre nature of the situation for fostering unwanted responses.

She listened carefully at the bathroom door before pushing it open into the adjoining bedroom. She was fully dressed, bathrobe on for good measure, but in fact she need not have worked herself up into a lather because he wasn't in the bedroom. The vast four-poster bed, bigger than a normal king-sized bed, was untouched.

She wasn't about to hazard a peek outside to see what he was doing or even whether he was still in the suite. She might be covered from head to toe but there was something about being dressed in pyjamas…

She dived into the bed, burrowed down so far to one side that she was inches away from tumbling off, hunkered down for the long haul and eventually fell asleep.

When she woke, daylight was doing its best to wriggle past the floor-to-ceiling curtains, which were still tightly drawn.

And Leo was nowhere to be seen, although his side of the bed had definitely been slept in.

She had no idea when he had got into bed and no idea when he had got out of it. It was after nine and she freshened up in a rush, changing into a summery dress, a cheap and cheerful addition to her wardrobe, and a pair of canvas espadrilles. She combed her hair loosely over one shoulder so it fell in soft waves and tentatively left the sanctuary of the empty bedroom.

Leo had been on the verge of waking her because time was moving on but, whilst he rarely suffered from jet lag, he accepted that she might need to sleep off the disruption to her body clock.

He was also strangely reluctant to venture into the bedroom.

By the time he had finally made it to bed, she had been fast asleep, her breathing soft and even. As his eyes had adjusted to the darkness, he could see that she had kicked off the duvet, just as he could see that her prim and proper top had ridden up and, from the angle in which she was lying, he could just about make out the soft swell of the underside of her breast.

He had felt like a voyeur.

Riveted to the spot, he had felt himself harden and, for the first time in his life, he had been unable to control his wayward libido as he had remained glued to the spot, staring at that sliver of pale skin, barely visible at all.

He had seen more of the naked female form than most men but he couldn't recall the last time he had been held captive by a glimpse of a breast.

Thinking about those few seconds, when he had barely been able to breathe, was enough to ensure he remain just where he was, at the desk by the window, waiting for her to emerge.

'You're up.' He pushed himself away from the desk and folded his hands behind his head.

She looked fresh and very, very young. Her pale hair flowed over one shoulder and caught the sun pouring through the huge windows, brightening the strands to a silvery white. She looked wholesome and sexy at the same time, although he was certain that she was utterly unaware of how appealing the combination was.

* * *

'I'm sorry I overslept. How long have you been up?'

'Three hours.'

'You should have woken me.' But she was relieved that he hadn't. She shied away from thinking about him shaking her until she opened drowsy eyes and looked at him, both in the same bed, warm from their shared body heat. 'I'm ready to go now, anyway.'

'Breakfast?'

'I'm not hungry.' She was starving but nobly decided to ignore her hunger rather than risk those cool, assessing eyes watching her as she tucked into a plate full of food.

'Sure?'

Sammy nodded, walking towards her handbag, which she had left in the sitting area on a chair. She stole a sideways glance at him as he rose elegantly to follow her to the door, casting a last look at the suite before opening the door for her.

She could see why he was taking her shopping. Next to him, her clothes shrieked *bargain basement* and whilst he really didn't seem to mind what kind of clothes she chose to wear, he certainly cared about the price of them.

Outside, she breathed in the heat, revelling in

the sun as it poured down on her shoulders, and, as they were ferried to the most expensive shopping street in the city, she looked left and right at the enormous diversity of the architecture.

Old and new jostled side by side. Coffee shops spilled onto pavements. There were elements of the past in the gracious Victorian buildings and arcades and elements of the ultramodern in spacious glass and chrome buildings that housed offices and shops.

The yellow taxis and glimpses of trams held her rapt attention because it was all so different in ways she couldn't quite put her finger on.

They entered an ornate arcade and he took her hand in his, linking his fingers with hers.

It didn't matter how many times she reminded herself that this was a business arrangement, she still couldn't stop herself from reacting to him and she was doing it now. Heat flooded her body and she knew that her face was red because all she could focus on was the feel of his cool fingers entwined with hers.

They hit the first shop, which, under normal circumstances, would have been way out of her price range. She didn't need to peruse the racks of clothes to establish that. She could tell at a glance from the lack of price tags and the elegant glacial beauty of the two shop assistants.

It was a large boutique, white and clinical, with a high-tech spiral staircase leading to an upper area.

Sammy hesitated by the door and felt him gently tug her in. 'Where's the excitement?' he murmured, leaning down, his breath warm against her ear.

'I'm not sure this is the sort of place that would stock anything I would like...'

'You haven't looked.'

'I can tell from the racks.' She smiled weakly at the saleswoman whose eyes briefly scanned her then moved on to Leo.

'Nonsense!' He firmly ushered her forward and Sammy watched, entranced, as he charmed the blonde beauty. Somewhere along the line, she got the impression that the other woman had recognised him, although, of course, it would have been totally out of order for her to have said anything. The actress he had dated was world famous. It wouldn't have surprised her if half of Melbourne recognised him.

'Now, darling...' he turned to her, dark eyes shielded '...take your pick.' He leaned down and gently cupped the side of her face in his hand, his fingers grazing her hair, which was as soft as silk and smelled of flowers. He lingered for a few seconds, startled by how much he was enjoying the feel of it, slippery under his fingers. 'If you feel the clothes here are a little too modern or revealing for you, then say the word.'

She was only twenty-six years old but he made her feel like a granny. Who could blame him, though? There was no denying her outfits had an old-fashioned flavour about them. It was brought sharply home to her just how much she had grown accustomed to hiding her figure behind baggy and unrevealing clothes. Comfort dressing was obviously a habit that she had become used to.

The soothing, patronising tone of his voice got her back up and she pursed her lips before smiling tightly at the shop assistant.

'Why don't you go and have a wander?' She reached up on tiptoe to cup his face just as he had done hers, going one step further and pressing her lips against his cheek. 'You don't want to spend your time sitting here looking at your watch while I try on outfits, do you? That'll be really boring for you.'

The show of loving familiarity was all for the benefit of their attentive spectators but Sammy still wasn't prepared when he curved both arms around her and drew her closely against him, angling her so that their bodies were neatly pressed together, his legs squarely planted apart to accommodate her between them.

Breathless, Sammy's eyes widened. Her whole body tingled and she was aware of herself, of every tiny pore and every strand of fine hair on her skin, in a way she had never been in her life before.

She shivered, as helpless in his embrace as a leaf being whipped along in a force ten gale. Instinctively, she leaned into him, overwhelmed with a sudden craving that shook her to the very core. This was much more than a kiss—this was the feel of his hard masculinity against her and it sent flames of desire licking through every part of her body.

Panicked, she flattened her hands against his chest but she wasn't allowed to push him back.

With a deep-throated growl of masculine satisfaction, Leo kissed her.

He wasn't into public displays of any sort, least of all when there was an audience, and there was very much an audience in the shop. Indeed, he had heard the sound of the door opening as more people entered but even that was not sufficient incentive to tear himself away from her.

What had started out as a little lesson to teach her that if she wanted to touch him to make a point then he was going to touch her right back to make an even bigger point had turned into something altogether different.

Way too different.

He drew back, releasing her abruptly, and it took a few seconds for his sudden withdrawal to register and, when it did, Sammy stepped smartly back, shaken to the core.

How had that happened? How had she *let* it happen? For a few long, long moments it had felt as though that kiss were the real thing, as though he were a real boyfriend. She just hoped that he hadn't sensed it. She smiled brightly at him but her eyes were unfocused.

Leo was looking at her narrowly. Had she intended to draw him into that kiss? His instinct was to have said no, but the way she had responded, throwing herself into it…

He had felt the yielding softness of her body beneath the cheap cotton dress, had felt the fullness of her breasts pushing against him. She had known just how to get to him with that little teasing taunt, just how to up the ante so that, for a minute there, he had well and truly lost sight of the fact that she wasn't one of his lovers.

She made a big song and dance about not liking the world of money, paparazzi and ur told luxury into which she had been thrown but he knew women and he had never met one whose head hadn't been turned by the glimmer of what his money could buy them. In fairness, most of them had needed no persuasion to kick back and enjoy what he could give them, but because she had started reluctant didn't mean that she would end up that way.

He hoped she wouldn't start getting ideas because that would be inconvenient.

And, just in case she *did*, even if the thought was just a shadow, a barely formulated shadow at the back of her brain, then he would have to cool the shows of ardour.

Certainly no more loss of self-control, which was what had regrettably happened just then.

'I like the way you're learning to play to the audience,' he murmured, low enough for her to hear and with an intimate smile that would convey to anyone who might be looking that sweet nothings were being whispered. Typical of a couple besotted with one another.

'Learning to play... Yes, well.'

'You're a quick study.' He dealt her a slashing smile and she smiled tightly back. 'No more cold war. No more protesting...I like it. It'll make this a whole lot easier.' He stood back and smiled at the saleswoman, who was managing to keep her distance without losing her quarry. 'Take care of her.' He gave her a little reassuring squeeze and waited until the blonde had approached them with an ingratiating smile.

'Darling—' Sammy looked up at him with a smile that oozed sugary sweetness '—don't make me sound so helpless!' She patted his cheek and their eyes met—hers blue, pushing the boundaries, his dark, knowing just what she was up to.

'I can't think of anyone less helpless than you,' Leo murmured with heartfelt sincerity. 'I'll return for you in an hour. Think that will be long enough for you?'

'Oh,' Sammy said breezily, 'I might have bought the entire shop by then!'

Their eyes tangled and she could see exactly what he was thinking.

Bought the entire shop? Hardly. You don't like shopping, you don't care about clothes... You'll head for the least daring racks and you'll be done in under fifteen minutes.

Sammy smiled. 'I think,' she said slowly, batting her lashes and frowning in a faraway manner, finger tapping the side of her mouth, head tilted to one side, 'I might actually need a littl' longer. Why don't we meet at Giles King's fices at three?' Was this what being ass with a man was like? It felt good, particularly when Leo frowned, caught on the back foot by a suggestion he hadn't anticipated.

It dawned on her that he was accustomed to calling the shots in every single area of his life. As far as he was concerned, he was paying her for her participation in this charade and he didn't expect her to do anything but follow his lead. She smiled brightly at him.

'You don't know where his offices are,' Leo pointed out.

'I think I'm smart enough to make my way there. I know the name of his firm.' She turned to the blonde, who was watching this exchange with fascinated interest. 'Men. They really *do* like to think of us as the weaker species, don't they?'

'I would never dream of being so cavalier where you are concerned, my sweet.' Leo wasn't sure whether to be amused by these antics, impressed by her ingenuity because she was putting on a show of loving familiarity that would have taken some beating, or uneasy because he wasn't on familiar ground and he had no idea where she was heading with this show of independence.

Then he relaxed.

Where could she possibly be going? As always, he had everything under control and, in the meantime, well, who ever said that life had to be predictable *all* of the time?

He thought that he might just start enjoying the next week and a half...

CHAPTER SIX

IT WAS A mad rush. Who knew that choosing some clothes and having bits and pieces done could actually take up so much of a person's time?

She'd whizzed through the shop, enjoying the heady feeling of having the snooty saleswoman bend over backwards to make sure she got exactly what she wanted.

Before they'd left the hotel, with Sammy still in protest mode at being told that her clothes were too cheap to be seen in when she was supposed to be engaged to him, he had urged her to buy whatever she wanted.

He already had details of her bank account and he had told her that if she didn't want him handing over his credit card to a salesperson because it went against her feminist instincts then she was free to use her own—he would ensure sufficient money was deposited into her account to cover all costs. He'd named a sum that had stunned her into silence and had shrugged when she had told him that she wouldn't know how to spend that amount of money because surely a few items of clothing couldn't cost very much.

Her plan had been to select the least outrageously expensive items of clothing and, likewise, the least flamboyant.

Plans, she discovered, could change in a heartbeat.

At the end of forty-five minutes in the boutique, and another forty-five minutes in two other boutiques farther along in the shady, exclusive arcade, she was weighed down by several bags, and two hours after that the hands holding those bags had been manicured and the feet shod in some rather delightful sandals, which were far more attractive than her canvas shoes and the hair... She felt like a million dollars.

But it had been an almighty rush. She hadn't been able to stop for food and, without breakfast, her stomach was intent on reminding her that sustenance was a lot more important than appearance.

And, for the first time in her life, Sammy didn't agree. She just had time to dash to the hotel, dump all the bags, change clothes and make sure she looked the part before she was back out to the car, which was on permanent standby just for her.

Now, with barely seconds to spare, she gazed at the graceful Victorian building that housed the law firm Leo was using to represent his interests.

Drawing in a deep breath, she purposefully strode towards the grey brick building, checked in at reception and was shown towards a conference room on the first floor.

Tension knotted her stomach. Nerves at the thought of the meeting that lay ahead and nerves at the new look she was sporting and how that new look would be received.

Did she look silly? she wondered.

She had felt so confident in the shop but then the saleswoman was in the business for a reason; she was adept at flogging very expensive clothes to women and part of her tactics would involve lavish praise and over-the-top compliments.

She told herself that instead of focusing on her silly clothes she should focus instead on what really mattered, which was the fate of a five-year-old girl whose life could be changed forever by what went on in that conference room.

This wasn't her. This person in shiny, expensive new clothes, seeking other people's approval and admiration. This wasn't her and it wasn't how she had been brought up!

Chin up, priorities firmly back in place, she took a deep breath and confidently entered the room, brushing past the young girl who had stepped back, holding the door open for her.

She only faltered for a second.

The room was absolutely enormous and there was nothing old-fashioned about the decor. A long, sleek table, so highly polished that it was as reflective as a mirror, dominated the central area, long enough to seat twenty people comfortably. To the back was a small circle of chairs and one wall was taken up with a white screen for presentations. There was a laptop in front of every chair. By the window, a sideboard, of the same highly polished wood as the conference table, housed coffee and tea-making facilities and plates of biscuits and tiny cakes, none of which appeared to have been touched.

Sammy took in all of this in a matter of seconds but, even as she was absorbing the surroundings, she remained entirely focused on the people sitting at that long conference table.

Leo easily dominated the group of eight. He

was sprawled back in his chair, which he had pushed away from the table, and his face was thoughtful and shuttered. He looked exactly like what he was—a lean, dangerous predator out to win.

But her eyes lingered on him for only a few moments because almost immediately she noticed the woman sitting directly opposite him and she knew, without having to be told, that this was Gail Jamieson.

She was small. Even sitting, Sammy could tell that she was no taller than five-two, maybe less, and she was the sort of woman who made jaws drop and caused heads to turn.

Her hair was a big bouffant and very blond, and her face tried desperately to belie her age, but the work she'd had done, rather than making her seem younger than her years, had somehow managed to age her.

Her eyes were wide and unblinking, her skin unnaturally line-free and her lips were pillowy and painted a bright fuchsia-pink, perfectly matching the colour of her formal suit which, likewise, matched her high stilettos.

She sought Leo, who had risen to greet her, and when he enfolded her in a brief embrace she wanted to stay there because she knew that the second she was released she would be in the firing line of Gail and her bank of representatives.

She had come out to play hardball and she wasn't going to pretend otherwise.

The conversation, the discussion of technicalities, voices being raised, Gail stridently talking over her lawyer and Leo responding coldly and with the sort of utter self-composure that should have been seen as a warning of armoury ready and poised for action passed in a blur and before she knew it the meeting was over.

As Sammy followed Leo—who was talking in a low, urgent voice to one of his lawyers—out of the room, Gail strode towards her.

'Funny,' Gail said, tugging Sammy to a stop, 'Sean never mentioned you when he spoke about his stepbrother.'

'Er…'

'And he spoke about Leo *a lot*. But never mentioned you. Not once. Funny that, wouldn't you say?'

'Why is it funny?' Sammy finally found her voice. She darted a look at Leo, who had not noticed that she had been held back. He had his hands in his pockets and she could see from his body language that he was one hundred per cent focused on whatever was being said to him.

'Because...'

Bright pink nails dug into Sammy's arm. When Sammy looked down she was skewered by light blue, unblinking eyes.

'Because he followed everything Leo did, and I mean *everything*. Knew who Leo was going out with almost before he was going out with them! But he never mentioned you. Not once. So I'm just curious as to how it is that Leo's suddenly engaged to be married. To someone he didn't know from Adam two months ago.'

'Love.'

Leo's voice was deep and dark and held just the tiniest hint of menace.

Sammy felt his arm around her waist and she leant into him, relieved beyond belief that he had interrupted what showed promise of being a difficult exchange.

'Ever experienced that, Gail? Or has the love of a good deal always won out over the love of a good man?'

Gail's lips pursed. Her ample bosom heaved. Every strand of heavily dyed blond hair seemed to bristle with rage.

'Over my dead body,' she spat, 'are you going to get the kid. And don't think that you an fool me into thinking that you're suddenly

Mr Respectable because you happen to show up here with some woman wearing an engagement ring.'

'I hope this isn't the sound of you spoiling for a fight,' Leo drawled. 'Because I don't like fighting but if I have to, I always emerge the winner.'

The pack of lawyers had disappeared, shooting off in separate directions.

'I've brought that kid up like she was my own!'

'Then I shudder to think what sort of upbringing your daughter was subjected to,' Leo informed her coldly. 'From what I've unearthed about you, a life of alcohol with a revolving door of unsuitable younger men hardly sounds like a woman who should have possession of a child.'

'Adele relies on me. I'm all she's known since she was born. Louise and Sean had their problems and I had the kid in my care more regularly than they did.'

'I have neither the inclination nor the time to get into an argument with you. If you want a fight, then fight through our lawyers. Don't ever let me find you trying to sideline my fiancée into any sort of conversation or, wo trying to intimidate her in any way whatsoever. Do you read me loud and clear?'

He hadn't bothered to look in Gail's direction when he said this and his voice was calm and perfectly modulated but, even so, Sammy felt a shiver of apprehension on behalf of the other woman should she decide to ignore the warning.

And Gail must have felt the same. Her bravado evaporated as they stepped back outside into the sweltering heat and the pulsing throng of people in shorts and tee shirts.

'I don't want to fight either.' Her voice was plaintive. 'If it comes to it, I just want what's fair for me and all the time I've put in with the kid. If it weren't for me…'

'I've already heard that tale of self-sacrifice.' Leo's arm was still draped possessively over Sammy's shoulders and he was looking at Gail now, through narrowed eyes. 'It failed to impress me the first time and it fails to impress me now.'

Sammy found that she had been holding her breath and she expelled it in one long, shuddering sigh of relief as the older woman merged into the crowds, a dollop of bright pink that was ·isible as she weaved along the pavements, fi- ·ly vanishing round a corner.

'Wow,' she said weakly. 'She's a force of nature.'

'She's an idiot for thinking she can win this.'

'She scared me,' Sammy confessed. 'I understand now why you felt you had to show up here with me in tow. I thought you had been exaggerating.'

His arm was still around her and she was suddenly self-conscious of how she looked. She had been talked into a long skirt that was light and fell beautifully to her ankles in various tie-dyed shades of apricot and grey. It was the height of modesty but the top twinned to go with it lovingly curved over her full breasts, dipping to expose just a hint of cleavage. The overall effect was one that made her look sexy and respectable at the same time. She had twirled in front of that mirror in the boutique and marvelled that she even had the ability to pull off a look like that.

She had thought that she would be excruciatingly self-conscious walking into that room in the lawyer's office but, in fact, she had barely been aware of what she was wearing.

'I hadn't expected her there.' There had been other things Leo hadn't been expecting, the way his *fiancée* looked in that outfit being one of them. She'd walked into that room ar every head had turned in her direction and his stomach had clenched as he'd taken in those darting, quickly concealed looks of appreciation from the men in the room. Including his own top lawyer who was fifty if he was a day, short and balding. Hope, he had thought grimly, certainly sprang eternal. Which hadn't made him any the less annoyed.

'I think—' he found his eyes straying to the sway of her heavy breasts and had to force himself to look away '—she decided that if she caught everyone on the hop then she might have the element of surprise.'

As if by magic, their car was pulling to the kerb, slowing for them to hop in, which was a blessed relief because it was so hot and humid. The long skirt was far cooler than trousers or anything shorter or tighter, but Sammy had still started perspiring within moments of leaving the lawyer's air-conditioned office.

Resting against the seat with her eyes closed for a couple of seconds, Sammy then turned to look at Leo. 'I barely took in what was going on. I was very nervous.'

'Legal back and forth,' Leo said drily. 'I've sat through enough meetings with lawyers to know that it's a very delicate rally that gets played in any situation where two sides are trying to meet.'

'*Are* you trying to meet? I mean—in the middle with Gail?'

Leo dealt her a cool sideways smile. 'I'm prepared to make some concessions. Louise and Sean made lousy parents and there's some truth in what she says, that the care of Adele fell on her shoulders more than should have been necessary. I've done extensive background checks on the woman, however. And, whilst she was technically in charge of her granddaughter, everything she says has to be taken with a pinch of salt. She's been demanding and receiving vast sums of money from my father and, well, you can see for yourself where some of that money has gone. There have been some plastic surgeons rubbing their hands in glee every time she's phoned to make an appointment. I know down to the last penny where the money's gone.' He shrugged. 'But if she doesn't put up a fight, then I'm willing to leave her with some cash.'

'She doesn't believe that this is a real engagement,' Sammy mused cautiously.

Her body tensed then flamed as he ran his eyes very, very slowly over her. She hadn't thought he'd noticed what she was wearing and then she'd decided that it wasn't her place to feel disappointed if he hadn't commented because there was no reason for him to. He' noticed. It was there in the heat of his brooding, fabulous eyes. By the time he had finished his leisurely inspection of her, her face was bright red and she would have told him in no uncertain terms that *looking at her like that* wasn't part of the arrangement except she had enjoyed every heat-filled second of that visual appraisal.

'Maybe she had her doubts when the news was first broken to her that I was no longer going to fit into the role of inveterate womaniser and unsuitable guardian which she had hoped for... Maybe she showed up here today with the express purpose of making sure her lawyers got on board with her way of thinking...but I think it's fair to say that after today...'

'I know what you're saying,' Sammy told him, breaking eye contact to find that the palms of her hands were slippery with perspiration and that had nothing to do with the temperature in the car. 'You were right. It would have looked peculiar if I had been wearing my department store clothes. Especially given that the woman looks as though she would be able to tell designer from fake without any trouble at all.'

'So good thinking. You chose just the right mix of daring and prudish. No one could doubt that you were a respectable teacher with just the right amount of sex appeal.'

'To attract a man of your high standards?' He'd noticed her but only insofar as she had chosen the right clothes for the job at hand. She gave a tinkling laugh that implied that she knew exactly what he meant.

'You're putting words into my mouth.' He wondered whether she was aware of just how incredibly erotic that alluring mix of daring and prudish actually was. He had given his lawyer some background details on her so they were all predisposed to think of her as highly respectable, moral, responsible—a shining example of just the sort of woman any man would bring home to his mother.

That said, had she looked too much like the moral, respectable teacher, they would all have been a bit bemused because how could a guy reasonably go from an actress whose face graced billboards to a teacher who was camera-shy and modestly dressed? Gail was astute. She would have sniffed out a phoney from a hundred paces and Sammy, resentful in borrowed clothing, would have been easily sniffed out. Better she be comfortable than bristling with transparent resentment.

But her choice of dress had been nothing short of inspired.

When they arrived back at the hotel he suggested dinner at one of the several excellent restaurants in the hotel. She could take her pick.

Sammy had forgotten all about her hunger pangs. Now, they resurfaced with a vengeance and no sooner had they sat down and bread was brought to them than she tucked in. To heck with pretending that she had the appetite of a sparrow, she thought.

'I'm ravenous,' she confessed, resisting the urge to help herself to more bread. 'What were you talking to your lawyer about? When we were leaving?'

'I don't think I've ever heard any woman admit to being ravenous.'

'I used to try dieting when I was younger but I gave up after a while. If you're hungry, I don't see the point of starving yourself.'

Sammy thought that since theirs was a phoney relationship based on necessity on both sides, there was no need to try and be someone she wasn't. She'd been out with guys in the past and she'd always been conscious of trying hard to be as ladylike as possible, which, in restaurants, had meant ordering healthy salads and dishes with weird ingredients that sounded good for you. But she wasn't out to impress Leo and he certainly wasn't open to being impressed by her. For him, she was a means to an end. She didn't have to edit her personality at all. She was the hired help. He touched her when he had to and when he looked at her, the way he had done just then, his dark eyes lazy and speculative, the only thing he was speculating about was how convincing she would be in her choice of clothing and whether there was anything else she could do to make sure he got what he had come to get.

'Watching their weight is part of some women's livelihoods.' He was fascinated by the enthusiasm with which she was working her way through her hearty starter of aubergine *parmigiana.*

'Of course it's important to be healthy. This is delicious. I don't do much eating out in expensive restaurants. On a teacher's salary, cheap and cheerful is usually all I can afford, and especially with the money problems Mum's been having.'

'As you know, my father offered her money countless times.'

'She's proud. She would never accept anything from your dad. I was surprised when she seemed to be all for this charade, though.

think it's a relief for her to know that I'll be getting something I've wanted for a really long time out of it and that it's not just about making sure that the mortgage is paid off.'

Plates were cleared. Wine was poured. She looked the most relaxed he had seen her since they had arrived in the country and he assumed that that was because the first steps had been taken towards resolving what they had come for.

The wine was also having its effect. She was on her second glass. He didn't think that she would be someone accustomed to drinking much alcohol.

Funny, he had known her for a long time and yet he felt as though he was getting to know her for the *first* time.

She had ordered a pie for her main course. It arrived with much fanfare and he couldn't help grinning as she tucked into it, taking a few seconds first to appreciate the mouthwatering beauty of the golden pastry and the rich red wine gravy bubbling through the crusty lid.

Sammy could feel his eyes on her but when he spoke it was to say, pensively, 'I'm beginning to realise that a woman who doesn't enjoy her food is probably not a woman worth going ut with.'

'What do you mean?' Sammy looked at him, her wide, bright blue eyes startled.

'There's something extremely sensual about food, wouldn't you agree? About someone who appreciates the pleasure of eating.'

Confused, Sammy, fork poised in mid-air and mouth half-open, was excruciatingly aware of Leo watching her as she ate a mouthful of the delicious beef and celeriac pie.

Leo watched her. It was an intoxicating sight. She was so unlike any woman he had ever been attracted to before. He could imagine that she was the sort of woman who came with all sorts of fairy-tale daydreams and unrealistic fantasies about happy-ever-after and soulmates. The sort who secretly collected bridal magazines and dreamed of having a dozen kids. A woman who came fully equipped with high moral values, which was why, he was forced to concede, she was so disapproving of him.

Disapproving but not immune.

With instincts that barely registered on any kind of conscious scale, Leo knew that.

It was there in the tide of colour that flooded her cheeks whenever he looked at her for a second longer than was strictly necessary.

Like now.

It was there in the way she lowered her eyes

and half turned away when she was caught looking at him.

And it had been there in her reaction to him every single time he had touched her.

She'd quivered, as if her whole body had suddenly come alive with an undercurrent of electricity over which she had no control.

Sammy cleared her throat and frantically tried to find something innocuous to say to break the sudden electric tension stretching between them.

'You…you were going to tell me what you were chatting to your lawyer about. When Ms Jamieson got me to one side. Um…'

'Was I?'

'Stop…stop looking at me like that.'

'Like what?' Leo raised his eyebrows in amused query.

Squirming because she was so out of her comfort zone, Sammy licked her lips nervously and looked away. 'Is there something you want to say about, um, about the way I look?'

'Yes,' Leo said gravely and Sammy's eyes flew towards him in sudden consternation.

'You said that my choice of dress was…that you liked what I had selected to wear.'

'Do you want honesty from me?'

'I don't know. Maybe not.' Sammy was blushing furiously.

'Okay.' Leo shrugged.

The conversation resumed on less contentious matters. Leo had been to the country several times, although only to Melbourne twice, and over the rest of the meal he proved a witty companion, full of interesting anecdotes about the places he had been. She truly began to appreciate the extent of his vast wealth as he told her about the properties he owned, scattered across the globe. She listened, asked questions and kept thinking, *did she want his honesty?* What did he think he had to be *honest* about?

'You might as well tell me,' she said in a rush, putting down her fork next to the chocolate brownie dessert she was halfway through.

Leo had known that sooner or later she would ask him to explain what he had meant, although if she hadn't he had resolved not to push the issue. He was attracted to her and there was a danger in that situation. He had agreed to this charade, and to his father's choosing her as a candidate to help pull it off, because he had known that she would be a safe proposition. Sex complicated things and he had not wanted complications. Eventually persuaded by his father to undertake this mission, he had come to the conclusion that in and out as fast as possible would be his approach.

Complications of any sort were to be avoided at all costs.

He signalled for the tab to sign but didn't take his eyes off her face. 'There is a small bar area farther along from the restaurant. They serve very good coffee.'

Sammy nodded. 'Just say what you have to say,' she half pleaded, tripping along beside him as he led the way to the cosy sitting area which, presumably, he had used before when he hadn't been in the suite with her. It was a perfect place to work in peace. Secluded, quiet, tucked away in a spot that was far from noise and crowds.

The fact that he was shying away from telling her what he had to tell her said something. It said that he knew she wouldn't be happy with whatever it was he had to say. Maybe his lawyer had said something to him during that little chat they had had when the meeting had come to a close.

She felt like a trainee about to be told that she hadn't, unfortunately, passed her probation because her work had not been up to scratch.

'When I agreed to do this—' he waited until she was sitting and then sat opposite her, adjusting his chair to accommodate the length of his body '—I decided that you were as ideal as it got for the job.'

'I know.' Defensiveness had crept into her voice. 'You knew how to get to me because of Mum. You knew that the money would be invaluable and you knew that my dream was to start my own freelance business so you had a good idea of what you could put down on the table to ensure I was left without much of a choice.'

'Spare me the victim speech, Sammy. You could have said no. We all have choices.'

'You thought I was convincingly *ordinary*,' she elaborated with grudging honesty. 'Have you decided that I'm just *too* ordinary? Because I don't know how I can overcome that. I can't turn into someone I'm not.'

Leo looked at her for so long that she began to fidget. 'You're not what I'd expected,' he said silkily. 'I'm seeing things I never saw before when we happened to bump into one another in the past.'

Sammy's mouth ran dry. She opened her mouth to say something but nothing emerged. She had no idea where he was going with this. She felt as though she had deliberately jumped into the path of an unstoppable train and would have to live with the consequences. If she could break eye contact she might be able to do something sensible like stand up and leave, but she couldn't seem to do anything but stare.

'There's something about you,' he murmured roughly, his sharp eyes taking in every small reaction in her expressive face. He'd never made a pass at any woman without knowing the outcome in advance. In fact, he'd seldom had to make passes at all. But this was different and he felt a swift adrenaline rush as he contemplated laying his cards on the table without fully knowing how she would react.

He wanted her. It made no sense and it was a nuisance, but she appealed to him in ways that were visceral and primitive and beyond his control.

He knew that he could keep trying to impose common sense but wouldn't it just be easier to scratch that itch? They were both adults and he suspected that she was as interested in exploring the chemistry between them that had blown up as he was. The fact that he wasn't *entirely* sure, instead of being a turn-off, had fired up his libido even more.

'Something about me?' Sammy squeaked.

'You're sexy,' Leo admitted in a roughened undertone. 'I can't seem to look at you without wondering what it would be like to take your clothes off.'

Sammy was having severe trouble breathing. Was he joking? Was this some kind of sadistic lead up to something really offensive he wanted to say?

'Of course I'm not,' she breathed shakily and he reached out and played with her fingers, toying with them and sending her scattered nerves every which way.

'And not just when you decide to make the most of your fantastic figure,' Leo assured her. 'So this has created a situation I hadn't banked on having to deal with.' He shot her a crooked smile that sent her blood pressure doing all sorts of irregular things. 'We're sharing a bed,' he told her bluntly, 'and I'm not going to beat around the bush. I want you. And I sense you want me, too.'

'Do you?' Sammy's voice was barely audible. 'I…I don't…'

'No?' He leaned forward suddenly, catching her by surprise. He reached out, hand curving at the nape of her neck, and drew her towards him. It was as if she had been hovering like a satellite circling a magnetic force which was warm and bright and irresistible and now that magnetic force was pulling her in and she wanted to go.

She could barely gasp before his mouth covered hers and his kiss was long and gentle and she fell into it with the ease of a hapless swimmer getting caught in a whirlpool. It just sucked her in. She closed her eyes, shifted closer, knew that she should push him back but couldn't find the strength.

He thought that she was sexy.

Her fingers trembled as they came into contact with his dark hair. This was the riskiest thing she had ever done in her entire life. Nothing else came close. He was so out of her league that they barely inhabited the same planet and yet here she was, kissing him and never wanting that kiss to stop.

She moaned softly.

This was her fantasy guy, the guy who had played a starring role in her adolescent daydreams.

A guy any woman would give her right arm to find herself in a clinch with—just like this one.

A guy who wasn't hers.

Cold, brutal reality asserted itself and she tore herself away from the embrace. She was shaking like a leaf. Her lips felt swollen and bruised from where he had kissed her and she had to resist wiping the back of her hand across them.

This wasn't about love or even affection. She was in a make-believe situation with a make-believe fiancé who would never have looked at her twice under normal circumstances.

Suddenly he found her sexy?

Hilarious. She had met him countless times over the years and he had never found her sexy on any of those occasions. Maybe his eyes had changed over time, maybe he needed specs.

Overcome with mortification at how easily she had leapt to that kiss, she was brutal with herself as she wrapped her arms around her body and looked at him.

'I don't want to...I'm not interested...'

'Sure about that?'

'And I think it's best we just put that behind us and remember that we're...remember that this isn't *real*.'

'The engagement isn't real,' Leo affirmed in a low, husky voice. 'My wanting to get you into bed, on the other hand, couldn't be more real.' He abruptly sat back and relaxed into his chair. 'But if you want to kid yourself that it's a one-way street, then that's fine by me. Moving on to what you asked me, I was talking to my lawyer about Adele. We meet her tomorrow.'

Head spinning from the change of subject, Sammy could only stare at him. He'd drawn her in only to suddenly drop her from a great height and he couldn't have been clearer in telling her that he might fancy her, and she still found that impossible to imagine, but he could take her or leave her at the end of the day. It was up to her.

Her brain struggled to focus on what really mattered.

'Tomorrow.'

'She will be delivered here to the hotel at lunchtime. It's been quite an achievement and Gail fought tooth and nail against it but she lost. She only found out when she spoke to her lawyer after the meeting today.'

He stood, waiting for her to follow suit. They were about to head for the bedroom, for the king-sized bed that would suddenly feel as big as a matchbox after what he had said. Her skin tingled at the prospect of getting into it with him.

'Don't worry,' he murmured, reading her mind or maybe her expression of full-blown panicked apprehension, as they headed for the bank of lifts to take them to their suite. 'I've never forced myself on a woman and I don't intend to start now. I have work to do when we get back and by the time I get into that bed you will already be sound asleep. Unless, of course, you decide that sex between two consenting adults who are attracted to one another is worth exploring...' He laughed when she pointedly ignored him and grazed his finger along her cheek, keen eyes watching the heat of her reaction.

'Sweet dreams,' he called as she disappeared into the bedroom but before she could shut the door on him. 'And don't forget—we're engaged... It's only natural to take things to their final conclusion!'

CHAPTER SEVEN

LEO HAD THROWN down his gauntlet. He'd been nothing but truthful when he had told her that being attracted to her had been an unforeseen curveball. She had skittered away like a Victorian maiden, shrieking with pious moral outrage, but then he'd kissed her and she had melted into his arms. He had needed no further evidence that she would be his.

Naturally, he wasn't going to pursue her.

He had been taken aback when they reached the suite to discover that she seemed to be sticking to her *hands off* moral high ground. She had stood in front of the bedroom door, like a bouncer on a mission to deter unwanted riff-raff, and informed him that she would be having a bath and perhaps he could make good on his promise to work until she had fallen asleep.

She had actually used the term *make good*, while he had stared at her as it had slowly dawned on him that she might just be sticking to her guns.

Leo had been genuinely confused. He'd taken the rash decision to bypass common sense and lay his cards on the table and, having done so, he had been gratified to find that the attraction worked both ways.

So where was the problem?

He had hit the bedroom an hour and a half after she had disappeared and had found her barricaded on her side of the bed, with two of the sausage-shaped cushions separating them.

He had woken at five-thirty, as he always did, wherever in the world he happened to be, and she had given no indication that she was awake. Her back had resolutely been turned to him and she hadn't moved a muscle as he'd made for the bathroom, showered, dressed and then exited the bedroom.

For the first time in living memory, Leo was finding it impossible to concentrate on work.

He kept looking at the closed bedroom door as the time ticked by. What was she doing? Was she up? Getting dressed? Abseiling down the side of the building in an attempt to get away from him?

He was distracted and he didn't like it. He was making himself a cup of coffee when the bedroom door finally opened so he remained where he was, lounging against the kitchen wall, cup in hand, watching her over the rim of it as he sipped his coffee.

'Get you some?' He raised the mug towards her and Sammy nodded politely.

Whilst she felt as though the bags under her eyes were as big as suitcases and just as obvious, he looked as fresh as a daisy.

And as drop-dead gorgeous as she'd hoped he wouldn't.

She'd heard him the second he had slipped out of the bed and every nerve in her body had tensed. Then he'd run his shower, not even bothering to shut the bathroom door fully behind him, and she'd sneaked a surreptitious glance at him, peeking out from where she was safely cocooned under the sheets and blanket. Her heart had almost stopped beating. He had taken his jeans into the bathroom with him and he was as indecently clad as any human could be whilst wearing trousers.

The top button was undone, the zip slightly down and, in the back light from the bathroom, she could make out every detail of his sinewy and completely bare upper half. The jeans rode low down lean hips and as he padded to the chest of drawers, quietly retrieving a tee shirt, she was treated to perfection in motion. He'd slipped the tee shirt over his head and she had squeezed her eyes tightly shut and drawn her breath in sharply because watching the ripple of muscle was just too much.

She had felt light-headed. How on earth was she going to be able to keep him at arm's length? No, more to the point, how on earth was she going to keep *herself* away from him at arm's length?

She'd never been so tempted by anyone in her entire life and she couldn't understand how it was that someone like him, who had absolutely *none* of the qualities she looked for in a man, would be the person to tempt her.

She had waited until he had shut the bedroom door behind him, then she had nodded off briefly before waking up and listening to make sure that he was well and truly absorbed in his work outside.

She'd felt like a thief, hiding out in a closet, forced to keep perfectly silent or else risk being caught red-handed with the family heirlooms.

Except what did she have to be sneaky about?

She'd kissed him back but then she'd pulled away and let him know in no uncertain terms that she was not up for a romp in the hay. She had stood her ground and she had retired to bed rather proud of herself.

The trouble was that her body refused to play along. She'd never found herself in the position of having to exercise denial when it came to a guy and denial physically *hurt*. Between her legs had throbbed and her breasts had ached. Her whole body had felt as though it needed to be touched and, lying in the darkness, her mind had been filled with images of him caressing her, taking her...

But Sammy knew that she couldn't allow herself to forget that this was a game. It would be dangerous to start blurring the edges between fiction and reality.

Consequently, she had dressed for the day ahead in the most sensible of the outfits she had bought.

It was going to be baking hot outside. She wasn't sure what the plans for the day were but she assumed that he would spend the morning working. At any rate, she would encourage him to do so, which would leave her free to explore the city until Adele was dropped off at midday.

She was wearing pale blue flip-flops, loose-fitting cotton trousers, also pale blue in colour, and a loose-fitting sleeveless top, patterned with a riot of tiny flowers that stopped at the waist so that when she moved a little sliver of tummy was visible. She had tied her hair in a high ponytail and escaped tendrils framed her heart-shaped face.

Leo took his time looking at her and when she blushed, he grinned and shrugged.

'I won't touch. At least not unless the occasion demands it.' He held his hands up in a gesture of mock surrender. 'But,' he drawled, 'I never promised that I wouldn't look.'

He turned around, fixed her a mug of coffee and sauntered towards her. Her blue eyes were wary but stubborn and he liked that.

'You shouldn't look at me like that,' Sammy said shakily.

'I can't help it.' He handed her the mug but he didn't move back. Instead, he remained towering over her, crowding her.

'I'm not going to sleep with you.'

'Did you hear me ask?'

'No, but…'

'I'm not going to pretend that I don't want to, though,' he said pensively, sipping the excellent coffee, amused when she shimmied away from him. He wondered whether she was scared that she might be driven to touch if she stayed too close to him.

His whole body went into overdrive when he

imagined her coming to him, unable to fight the force of their mutual attraction.

'What are your plans for the day?' Sammy thought that if she didn't change the conversation he would carry on looking at her with those brooding, amazing, fabulously sexy eyes and she would go up in flames.

'*My* plans?'

'I thought as we aren't due to meet Adele until lunchtime that you might want to get some work done.'

'Why would you think that?'

'Because you obviously have a lot on your plate. I mean, you don't get to bed until very late and you're up early so that you can catch up.'

'A wild number of misconceptions in that statement,' Leo said lazily. 'I'm my own boss. I'm not a hamster on a treadmill, running furiously for fear of getting left behind. And yes, I don't happen to need much sleep but I assure you that I would be more than happy to hit the sack early and get out of it late if the incentive was right...'

'Will you stop doing that!' But it turned her on. Why bother to pretend otherwise? She *liked* the way his eyes on her made her feel. She *enjoyed* the slow, crazy burn she got when he talked like that, saying things that made her feel sexy and feminine, which were two things she had never felt in her life before. He was the equivalent of a slab of wicked, wicked chocolate. You wanted it so much but you knew that you had to fight the temptation because one bite wouldn't be enough and it certainly wouldn't be good for you.

'I wouldn't dream of leaving you to your own devices today,' he said, pocketing his cell phone and heading towards the door. 'We'll get breakfast, then do some city exploring and get back here in time to meet Adele.'

Sammy knew when she was beaten. She hoped he wouldn't wage his devastating assault on her senses. She found herself fast-forwarding to conversations they might or might not have. She braced herself to keep pushing him back.

She was disproportionately disappointed when the morning passed with him being the perfect gentleman.

He held her hand but he didn't try to kiss her. He looked at her, but those looks didn't linger longer than necessary. She had expected to spend three hours rigid with tension but he seduced her into talking about herself and, afterwards, she couldn't imagine how he had done that.

How had he managed to bypass her guard?

'Are you nervous?' she asked as they were making their way back to the hotel.

'About what?' Leo looked at her with a frown. It had taken more willpower than he knew he possessed not to touch her.

'Seeing Adele.'

'The only thing I'm nervous about is this custody battle not going in my favour. My father wouldn't recover.'

'Have you spoken to him?' Sammy's voice softened for she was hugely fond of the elderly man.

'Two emotionally charged emails and one phone call where he sounded as though a nervous breakdown wasn't far away. This has to work out. There's no choice.'

'Do you have much experience of children?'

'Is that a necessity?'

'It helps.'

'I don't.' He turned to her as they entered the cool of the hotel lobby. 'So it's just as well that I have someone by my side who can make up for my shortfall, isn't it?'

He looked past her and then pulled her close to him and dropped a kiss on her head.

Sammy had followed his eyes and almost immediately her heart went out to the child sitting on one of the long grey sofas in the lobby, next to a man she recognised as one of the lawyers from the other side.

Adele was a pretty little thing, with long dark hair caught in two braids which ended in pink ribbons, neatly tied into bows. They matched her dress and her shiny patent plastic shoes. She was sitting ramrod straight, her hands folded on her lap and next to her was a bright pink bag. Not a backpack but a handbag. Her face was small and serious and she looked terrified.

Leo hadn't seen her for well over a year. Suddenly, the enormity of his undertaking was brought home to him. This wasn't a deal. There was no company involved, no stock market to follow in the wake of a deal, no factory that might or might not need to be closed, no redundancies to be handled and workforce to be relocated. This was a living, breathing child and he tensed.

Sammy felt it. He had faltered. No one would have noticed, but *she* did. She looped her arm through his without looking at him, took a deep breath and headed directly for the little girl who was primly sitting on the grey sofa.

'Hi.' She ignored the lawyer, who had risen

and taken Leo to one side so that they could have a confab. 'I'm Sammy.' She knelt down so that she was on eye level with Adele. She was accustomed to young children. She was comfortable around them and she knew how to make them feel comfortable around her. It was part and parcel of being a good teacher.

Leo watched her. The lawyer was busily telling him about the arrangements that had been secured for the day and the outcome of the long meeting they had the day before. Leo heard everything but his attention was riveted to the woman kneeling in front of the little girl. All her natural warmth was on show. She was very tactile, was resting her hand on Adele's arm, and he could see the way the child was being drawn into whatever she was being told.

Compared to her, his girlfriends of the past, with their frantic self-absorption, now struck him as somewhat brittle.

There was an earthy, engaging and entirely uncontrived sexiness about his fake fiancée that kept turning him on. He dragged his attention away to finalise details of handing Adele back to the lawyer and then, lawyer gone, he joined the twosome, standing above them until Sammy straightened.

Introductions were made. Adele stared at

him with huge navy blue eyes and noticeably cringed back.

'What now?' Leo asked roughly, on the back foot for the first time in his life.

Sammy gave Adele's hand a tiny reassuring squeeze. 'Leave it to me.' She stood on tiptoe and impulsively kissed the side of his mouth because he looked uncertain and weirdly vulnerable and she liked that. She liked knowing that, for the first time in his life, probably, he wasn't quite in control of a situation.

They had Adele for lunch and the remainder of the afternoon, and Sammy allowed the little girl to choose what she wanted to do. They lunched at a popular restaurant where everything was geared towards children, from what was on the menu to the colouring books and games they could enjoy while they waited for their food.

Then they went to the Melbourne Aquarium.

'Do you do stuff like this often?' Sammy asked casually at one point during the day, and Adele shook her head and whispered that sometimes Sarah would take her out but mostly she stayed in and played with her toys.

'Sarah?'

'The girl who looks after me,' Adele said. 'Nana Gail doesn't have much time because she goes out a lot and she's busy all the time.'

Leo tried to involve himself but he was so clearly making an effort that it had the opposite effect of scaring Adele away. The bigger the effort he made the more alarmed she seemed to get. And the more frustrated he became. By the end of the day, there was a tentative hug from Adele for Sammy and a polite handshake for Leo. Pink plastic bag dangling on her tiny wrist and feet beautifully turned out because, she had confided haltingly, she did ballet lessons three times a week because it suited her grandmother who met friends for early evening drinks then, she looked like a miniature queen politely bidding one of her subjects goodbye.

'Well, that was a complete fiasco,' was the first thing Leo said as they headed up to the suite. 'I need a drink. Actually, scratch that. I need several drinks.'

Sammy was on a high. She had had a wonderful time. She had been as nervous as a kitten about meeting the lawyers, about meeting Gail and about the whole pretend charade, and Adele had been a shining light, returning her to her comfort zone. And it had felt good to find herself in the leading role for the first time, rather than tumbling around on a roller coaster ride into which she had suddenly been plunged.

'It wasn't a fiasco,' she said, stepping into

the lift and then turning to him as they were whooshed up to their suite. 'It went really well.'

'It went really well for *you*,' Leo amended, lounging against the mirrored panel, thumbs hooked on the waistband of his jeans. 'You're obviously a natural when it comes to children.'

'It's my job. Besides, I really liked her. She's been through a rough time. That's why she's so quiet and scared. I can't imagine what it must have been like having two very young and irresponsible parents and then, when they're no longer around, having to cope with a grandmother who clearly doesn't particularly want her around.'

'You're really...' He looked at her, head tilted to one side until colour crawled into her cheeks.

'I'm really *what*?'

Leo opened the door with his key card and pushed it, stepping back so that she could brush past him. She smelled of sun and the outside— a flowery, healthy, clean, natural smell that filled his nostrils, making him want to take a step back and close his eyes.

'Caring.' He took up where he'd left off.

Over the years, he had heard all about her from his father, who was her number one fan. It had mostly gone in one ear and out the other. But he remembered things he had been told now, about how good she was at her job, how popular she was with her pupils, the sort of girl who took in stray animals and nursed them back to rude health. Privately, it had all sounded like the perfect description of a bore with whom he couldn't possibly have anything in common. Pious and saintly, which had always been the image he had been fed, couldn't have been further from the sort of person who could engage his attention.

But she was nothing like that image he had built in his head. She didn't set about drawing attention to herself like most women he knew were prone to doing, but she was still curiously capable of holding his attention in ways he didn't really get.

And she was naturally empathetic. He had seen that for himself with Adele today, if it hadn't already been apparent.

She was feisty but caring, argumentative and stubborn as a mule but had what it took to gain the trust of a suspicious five-year-old. She didn't strut her stuff and blushed like a teenager. He couldn't imagine anyone less likely to make a pass at him, even if she wanted to. She believed in true love and was seriously romantic.

In all respects, she managed to tick none of

the boxes that he had always thought counted when it came to women.

But the more he was in her company, the more turned on he was by her.

Sammy thought that he had succeeded in turning *caring* into *as boring as watching paint dry*.

'You mean I'm dull!' She laughed off the knot of hurt that tightened inside her.

He was pouring himself something from the well-stocked minibar and she accepted a glass of wine because she was still smarting from the *dull as dishwater* description she had read into his words.

It wasn't yet six-thirty. She guessed that the plan would be for them to go somewhere for dinner. After two nights, she no longer felt awkward about the whole sharing a bed situation. He seemed to have an amazing ability to detach. He might tell her that he found her sexy, but he didn't feel any compulsion to follow through.

Thank heavens, was what she firmly told herself.

'You're anything but dull.' Leo had opted for red wine over his instinctive choice of something a lot harder and he looked at her as he sipped it.

The day's outing had done great things to her satiny skin, which was fast acquiring a pale gold colour and turning her blond hair even blonder. The ponytail had disappeared at some point during the day and her hair now tumbled in curls and ringlets over her shoulders. She was the picture of health, the perfect image of someone who didn't care about what the weather was doing to her make-up or her hairstyle. Once he'd started staring, he found that he couldn't stop and he had to physically turn away and prowl towards the floor-to-ceiling window that overlooked a park that was bathed in the last of the sunshine.

'I just want to say…' He frowned and tried to locate the right words.

'What?' The wine was delicious and Sammy wandered to where he was standing and absently looked outside before turning her attention to him.

'I want to thank you.' His voice was gruff and she gazed at him, bewildered.

'Thank me for what?'

'You took charge today.' He drained his glass, twirled it thoughtfully between his fingers and then gently placed it on the squat glass table next to him. 'Quite honestly, I'm not sure how things would have gone if you hadn't been there.'

'You would have... You...er...'

'I can tell you're confused because you can't decide which of the many things I did today made just the right impression on Adele. You're spoilt for choice.'

Sammy blushed and laughed because he was incredibly endearing when he was being self-deprecating.

'You would have coped. I have a lot of experience when it comes to dealing with young children and you don't have any. I guess it was always going to be easier for me. I also don't have any emotional investment in the situation whereas you do.'

'That's a very generous take on the situation. I like that about you.'

'What do you mean?'

'You give the benefit of the doubt to people.'

'And you don't?' Her heart was beating like a jackhammer because the conversation was so personal. She liked the feeling of playing with fire. She liked not caring whether she got burnt or not.

'I really want to make love to you.'

Sammy froze. Her eyes widened and her

breathing slowed to a near stop. His voice was thick with intent.

'I mean,' Leo continued huskily, 'we could carry on pretending that there's nothing between us. I could work out here until I'm certain that you're asleep and then I can creep into the bed and wake up before you start surfacing from your beauty sleep and we can both kid ourselves that we haven't shared the same bed at all and that, even if we did, it doesn't matter because we're just two business associates on a job and that if there's some chemistry then we can choose to ignore that. I can make sure not to look at you for too long and only touch you when we're in public. I can pretend that I don't feel you tremble when I do touch you. I can pretend that you don't sigh softly when I kiss you. The alternative, however...'

He allowed that to stretch out into the silence between them while he continued to pin her to the spot with his eyes.

'This isn't real.' Sammy heard the desperation in her voice as she tried to cling to sanity.

'We're not really engaged,' Leo agreed in a roughened undertone. 'And we won't really be walking up the aisle with stars in our eyes. But *this*...' he cupped the side of her face with his hand and then caressed her smooth skin, dropping his finger to her mouth and tracing the outline of her lips '...*this* is real.'

'We shouldn't...'

'You're preaching to the converted,' Leo confessed with raw honesty. 'I know that making love isn't what either of us had planned. I know I'm probably the last guy in the world you would actively hunt down...' He wasn't even aware of leaving a pause after he said that but he was piqued when she didn't rush to fill it with a denial.

'I'm not the kind of girl who falls in bed with someone.'

'No.' Her skin was so soft and silky. It was torture trying to suppress his very natural urge to take and conquer.

'In fact,' she said awkwardly, 'I'm not the type of girl who has ever fallen into bed with someone.'

His hand stilled and he frowned as his brain tried to compute what she had just said. And failed. Was she admitting to being a virgin? A woman in her twenties?

'You're kidding.'

Sammy stared off into the distance. If her heart were to beat any faster she would be in danger of it cracking a couple of ribs. She'd always known that she would have to have this conversation with whatever guy she eventually fell into bed with, but in her head the conversation had never been with a man like Leo. In her head the conversation had always been with a kind, gentle guy who would clasp her hand and understand where she was coming from because he, like her, if not a virgin, would have been discriminating with his women.

Leo enjoyed women unabashedly. He took what he wanted, always drawn to the prettiest and the most tempting, and he moved on quickly from one to another.

The fact of her virginity was just something else that separated them.

Actually, there were so many things separating them that she could start counting now and probably not reach the end of the list by the time they left the country.

'Why would I be kidding?'

'Because…' Leo was lost for words. 'Because… How old are you?'

'Twenty-six.'

'You're *twenty-six* and you've *never* slept with a man?'

Sammy flushed but she wasn't ashamed of that and never had been. She'd never been part of any crowd, growing up, who had giggled and ticked off the days on a calendar before they could lose their virginity and, once she had left her teens behind, the subject had never arisen with her girlfriends. If anything, she had seen enough broken hearts from friends who had become hopelessly involved with the wrong type of guy to have known that when she did decide to sleep with a man it would be with the right man.

What a joke, as it turned out.

Because she wanted to sleep with *this one* and *wrong* didn't begin to describe the category he fell into.

'Why not?' Leo asked bluntly. He still couldn't get his head round that idea but now he was looking at her in a slightly different light. *A virgin?*

'Because it just never happened,' she muttered under her breath, red as a beetroot and furiously wishing she had never said anything. She should have just carried on keeping him at arm's length and not softened at that glimpse of vulnerability.

'I get it…' Leo said slowly, his beautiful mouth curving into a smile of lazy intent. 'You thought that sex was something you could control. You'd fall in love and sex would follow as a tidy little afterthought. You believed that love and sex came as a package deal…'

'I never said that.'

'But you're attracted to me and that doesn't compute.' He'd never experienced any woman fighting an attraction to him. 'You've discovered that lust doesn't necessarily go hand in hand with love, and you've found out that it's powerful enough to make minced meat of common sense. Welcome to the real world.'

'There's nothing real about what we have.'

'You can keep fiddling around with words, Sammy, but you still won't be able to turn the chemistry between us into something else because it makes you feel uncomfortable.'

'This is crazy!' she burst out, looking at him with agitation. 'It doesn't make any sense. It would be madness to…to…'

She didn't get to finish the sentence.

Because he pulled her towards him and kissed her and he kept on kissing her until all thought faded away and what was left was pure sensation.

CHAPTER EIGHT

AT THIS STAGE in the proceedings, Leo would have marked his boundary lines out very clearly. He didn't feel that he needed to with Sammy, though. She got them. She had entered this contract with her eyes wide open and she knew him for the man he was—a man who wasn't going to ever offer her anything but the gratification of a physical need.

She wasn't a woman rushing to climb into bed with him as a prelude to trying to stake a claim. She was a woman who had done her best to avoid climbing into bed with him and staking a claim was the last thing on her mind.

She wasn't losing her virginity to him because he was the man she had been looking for all her life. She was losing her virginity to him because, like a minnow caught in a riptide, she just couldn't help herself.

The chemistry between them, for all sorts

of reasons he couldn't understand, was over-powering.

'Sometimes crazy is good,' he broke away to rasp. Without giving her time to find an answer to that observation, he picked her up and she gave a soft little gasp because they were heading for the bedroom and that king-sized bed.

She'd definitely overestimated her ability to hang on to her self-control when he was around!

If they'd buried this and not brought it out in the open, she might have been safe but, as it stood...

She spread her hand flat against his chest and felt the hardness of muscle. If she stopped to think about whether it had anything to do with love or affection or wanting to discover more about her, then she would go mad. It was all about sex and lust and he was right—she had never predicted how powerful a physical urge could be.

He deposited her on the bed and then stood back and looked down at her with an expression of masculine satisfaction.

'Hot day out there...'

'Huh?'

'I'm thinking we should start with a bath. How does that sound?'

'Maybe we should just get it over and done with.' Sammy looked at him anxiously and he burst out laughing.

He raked his fingers through his hair and gazed at her with lively amusement. 'That's the first time any woman has ever said that to me. *Maybe we should just get it over and done with...*' He shook his head and dropped onto the bed to sit next to her and she scrambled up so that she was hugging her knees, her eyes wide with a mixture of apprehension and hot longing.

Both did unheard of things to his body. His erection was so hard it was painful. He had no idea how he was going to get through a leisurely bathing session but sating their needs fast and hard was going to have to wait.

'Is this the first time you've ever made love to a virgin?' she asked quietly and he touched her cheek briefly.

'It is, but don't be scared, Sammy. I'll be gentle. I just need to make sure of one thing— I need to know if this is really what you want.' His voice was utterly serious. This wasn't quite what she had expected. She had summed Leo up as the typical wealthy, good-looking businessman who could have any woman he wanted and so took without thinking of consequences.

She'd assumed that he was selfish sexually, happy to pick up and discard women without any thought to whether he left them with broken hearts or not.

His account of what had happened behind the scenes with Vivienne Madison had subtly changed that opinion but perhaps her opinion had been changing before that.

Assailed by a moment of confusion, her mind went blank for a few seconds and then she slowly began processing that the three-dimensional man was nothing like the cardboard cut-out she had had in her head.

'Really what I want?' she parroted weakly.

'You've spent your life saving yourself for the right man,' Leo told her roughly. 'I'm not the right man for you and I never will be. I'm not on the lookout for love—I don't have time for the complication of emotions. If I were to describe my ideal life partner, it would be someone whose view of the institution of marriage was similar to my own. A man like me would be no good for you any more than a woman like you would suit a man like me.'

Sammy hugged her knees tighter to her chest. She was being given an out. She looked at him, chin tilted mutinously at an angle. 'You were right,' she told him. 'I thought sex and love went together. I hadn't banked on being swept off my feet by…by…lust.'

Leo was impressed because it was brave of her to admit that. It would have been much easier to have buried her head in the sand, stuck it out here for the next week and then pocketed the money and put the whole thing down to experience rather than facing up to something she found uncomfortable and bewildering.

'Is that you telling me that you want this?'

Sammy nodded and he grinned. 'You're going to have to do better than that, Sammy.' He sifted his fingers through her hair and gently tugged her towards him. His kiss was long and deep, their tongues meshing, driving her wild.

'Let me hear you say it…' he encouraged, breaking apart to look at her.

'I…I want this.' Sammy felt heady and reckless. She felt as though she had one foot hanging off the side of a precipice. In a minute she would leap into the air and free fall. She was terrified and excited all at once.

'In that case, stay right where you are.'

He padded off to the en suite bathroom, where she heard the sound of the bath being run. When she thought about the two of them in that bath she shivered. But she wasn't going to back out.

Her mind was frantically trying to deal with images of them together when he reappeared at the bathroom door, leant against the door frame and gazed at her with his arms folded.

'Rule number one,' he drawled, 'is to relax.' He strolled towards her and she followed his lazy progress with wide blue eyes. 'Rule number two is to stop thinking that what we're about to do will be anything but exquisite. And rule number three...' he ran his fingers through her hair and gently tilted her face upwards so their eyes met, his reassuring, hers needing reassurance '...is that you trust me.' He stood back and held out one hand and she took it mutely and then he led her to the bathroom, where the bath was a mass of fragrant bubbles.

'Now...' Leo positioned her in the middle of the bathroom and stood back, gazing at her with the eyes of a connoisseur. It was an exaggerated pose, finger lightly resting on his mouth, head tilted back, eyes half closed, and she wanted to laugh, which relaxed her.

'What are you doing?'

'Where to start?' he murmured. 'With your top, I think...'

'No—no!' She hurriedly stepped back and hooked her fingers under the stretchy fabric. 'I can do that myself.'

'Should I turn my back and only look around when you're safely concealed under a metre of bubbles?'

'Hardly a metre!'

'You're not going to get away that lightly,' he teased, enjoying the novelty of a woman who wasn't flinging herself at him. He walked towards her and when she opened her mouth he gently placed one finger over her lips. 'Now, remember those rules of mine?'

Sammy nodded meekly.

'Okay. Let's focus on rule number three, which is *trust me*.' He lightly tapped her hands away from the top to replace them with his own and slowly, tantalisingly slowly, he pulled the top over her head, keeping his eyes on her face, and then he tossed it on the chair by the door.

Sammy's mouth was dry. 'I know I'm not exactly skinny,' she breathed huskily and he tutted under his breath. 'My breasts are way too big,' she continued, just in case she hadn't already made it perfectly clear that making love to her wasn't going to be like making love to one of his superslender models or waif-thin actresses, and not just because she was a virgin.

Leo was finding it very hard to step back from the searing urge to rip her bra off and feel those lush breasts for himself. The last thing his aching erection needed was a description from her about just how generous they were in size.

'You're perfect,' he ground out, briefly closing his eyes to get a grip.

Sammy would have launched into a question and answer session about his definition of *perfection* because she had eyes in her head and knew that *perfect* was the last thing she was, but he had slid his hands behind her back and was unclasping her bra.

She gasped and squeezed her eyes tightly shut as the bra joined her top on the chair. Her body was as rigid as a plank of wood but not for long, as he curved big hands around her breasts and then, slowly and expertly, rubbed his thumbs over the stiffened peaks of her nipples.

Leo wasn't sure he was going to be able to keep up the pretence of the sophisticated lover in control of the situation when he felt as though he was on the brink of exploding. He was hard as a rock and throbbing. When he looked down to those heavy, abundant breasts with their circular pink nipples, he could easily have been a horny adolescent on the verge of losing his virginity. That was how turned on he was.

He continued to massage them, to play with her nipples, while she moaned softly under her breath, as if a little embarrassed to be making any noise at all.

Her inexperience hit him like a dose of adrenaline and he fumbled, in a very uncool way, with her trousers, which he somehow managed to get down her legs without his usual aplomb.

She stepped out of them. Sammy's eyes were still squeezed shut and, whilst everything was melting, she just didn't quite know what she should do next. Her whole body went up in flames when she thought of those fabulous dark eyes scrutinising her body. She took a peek and daringly made some halting attempts to get him to the same state of undress as she was.

'Shh…' Leo murmured, as though she had spoken. He stayed her hand.

'This feels weird,' Sammy said shyly. Their eyes met and he nodded. He had never made love to a virgin in his life before. Had she ever seen a man naked? He was well built. Would his sheer size intimidate her? He stepped back and began undressing, his dark eyes fixed on her as she watched him with unabashed fascination. Without thinking, she had covered her breasts with her arm. It was curiously erotic.

Shirt off, he began unzipping his trousers.

Sammy couldn't take her eyes off him.

He was the most sensationally beautiful man she had ever seen and all of a sudden she knew, with some kind of unerring instinct, that she had been looking at him all her life. He'd never noticed *her*, but she had spent her life noticing *him*.

And now here she was...

She was so turned on that she had to briefly close her eyes and, even with her eyes closed, she could still see his image imprinted on her retina. Broad bronzed shoulders, muscled arms, narrow waist and washboard-hard stomach.

When she opened her eyes he was stepping out of the trousers and she gasped, her mouth forming a perfect oval, and Leo grinned.

'I can't remember the last time I had such a dramatic reaction from a woman at the sight of my naked body,' he drawled wryly.

Sammy's cheeks were burning. Her eyes flicked down to his substantial, impressive manhood and then back to his face. He was still grinning.

'Don't worry—' he read her mind without her having to say what was on it '—male and female bodies are engineered to fit together.'

He urged her into the bath. It was huge, big

enough for them both, but he knelt at the side and lavished his attention on her, taking his time as he soaped her, massaging her neck until her bones turned to water and then moving on to massage her breasts until she was so relaxed she just wanted to sigh and moan and enjoy the intense pleasure of his hands on her.

Her self-consciousness had disappeared some time between sinking into the hot water and hearing the sound of him lathering soap between his hands.

By the time his big hands were moving over her breasts, her legs were limp and her eyelids fluttered as he worked his way down her body, urging her to sit up so that he could soap her back, his thumbs pressing against her spine in a way that was quite, quite delicious.

'Enjoying?' he whispered and she nodded and muttered something that was meant to signify a resounding *yes*.

'Still nervous?' he questioned, and she flicked drowsy eyes at him.

'Not so much,' she confessed. 'You're good at this, aren't you?'

'I've never been in this position before. It's as new to me as it is to you.'

'But you have heaps of experience.'

'There's another rule I should have added,'

Leo mused. 'I should have added the *no chatting* rule.'

'I mean—' Sammy ignored him completely '—I always imagined that when I was, well, in this position... You know what I mean, that it would be with someone less...er...'

'There would be something a little weird about a guy in his mid to late twenties who was still a virgin. Or am I being a little fanciful here? Now, stop talking!'

His hands moved over her body, massaging gently, exploring gently, finding her inner thighs and separating them...also gently. His caresses were unhurried and measured and she physically felt herself relaxing more and more until all the apprehension had seeped out of her.

She received his finger with a shiver as it slid between her legs. Maybe it helped that she was covered in warm, sudsy water. Or maybe because the lighting was dimmed in the bathroom and her eyes were closed so that she couldn't see that lean, beautiful face. Or maybe she was just, weirdly, relaxed. She didn't understand how or why but she was. Everything was happening so slowly.

Leo stroked her between her legs, building up the rhythm. He knew that this would be achingly intimate for her, and he half wondered whether some kind of prudish instinct would kick in and she would push his questing hand away, but she didn't and he was inordinately pleased by that.

It mattered to him that she open herself to him and that was what she was doing. Her breathing quickened and her cheeks became flushed with hectic colour. She was moving in the bathtub, bucking ever so slightly so that the water lapped around her, enabling him to see the slick wetness of her big breasts rising and falling. He kept up his gentle but insistent rhythm until, with a deep groan, she arched up and spasmed against his finger.

Sammy was shocked and mortified at the way she had just *let go*. She had been so caught up in the waves of pleasure rolling over her that she would not have been able to stop herself if she had tried.

When she opened her eyes, he was smiling and she struggled up into a sitting position. 'I'm sorry...' She could barely get the words out. He stroked her face, stood up and helped her to her feet.

'You should be,' he admonished, 'because I'm so turned on I feel as though I'm about to explode. I had planned this bathing experience to be very long and very leisurely but I'm going to have to revise that plan.'

'Why's that?' She smiled shyly because she knew what he was saying and yet she could hardly believe it.

'Fishing?' Leo grinned, outrageously masculine in his nakedness. If he didn't have her, and have her fast, he wasn't going to be responsible for whatever his body decided to do.

'Yes,' Sammy confessed honestly. He helped her out of the tub and wrapped her in a towel and she was bemused to find herself suddenly settling onto the oversized bed—the same bed which had filled her with dread when she had first arrived.

Leo laughed. 'I like that,' he confided, and she looked at him with a puzzled expression. 'The way you have of saying exactly what's on your mind,' he elaborated. 'You don't care what impression you make.'

'And that's a good thing?' Sammy asked lightly.

'Refreshing. The women I date have always taken great care to say what they thought I wanted them to say.'

'I thought all men liked women who agreed with them.'

'Maybe,' Leo murmured, 'or maybe that's

just a lazy response. Now, enough talk.' He sank onto the mattress and guided her hand to his throbbing erection, drawing in his breath sharply as she wrapped her fingers around him.

She asked him what to do. She was anxious that he enjoy himself. Her frank honesty and hesitancy was refreshing.

'Don't worry about me,' he told her roughly. 'This is about *you*. I want this first time for you to be special. I want you to remember it forever.'

Sammy's heart swelled as he angled her underneath him, pinned both her hands together above her head with one hand and then instructed her to leave them there.

If he was as turned on as she was, then his whole body would be on fire, just as hers was, and yet he was willing to sublimate his urges so that he could take his time with her. He nuzzled the side of her neck and she wriggled and sighed, her eyelids fluttering as he then proceeded to work his way downwards, sprinkling a trail of delicate, feathery kisses along her collarbone, then lower to the soft swell of her breasts.

She opened one eye and the sight of his dark head, the intimacy of where it was placed just there by her nipple, made her stifle a squeak of edge-of-the-seat excitement.

She closed her eyes. She felt like the cat that nabbed the cream. His mouth edged down to her nipple and he suckled on it, drawing it in and teasing it with the tip of his tongue. Sammy groaned out loud. Her hands itched to burrow into his dark hair and propel him harder against her sensitive nipple but instead she clasped her fingers together and squirmed as he continued to send her body to heaven. She was still tingling between her legs and the tingling was building momentum, wanting satisfaction all over again.

He caressed her breasts, torturing her by taking his time as he explored first one then the other. He licked her nipples, traced them with his flicking tongue, nipped them and sucked them until she barely recognised the low, shuddering moans coming from her.

Those moans grew deeper when he cupped her between her legs and very gently pressed down in lazy circular movements.

Leo felt her impatience, felt her body yearning to receive him and he wanted nothing more than to yield to the siren call of desire, to satisfy his driving need to feel her tight and hot around his hard, painfully erect manhood.

It took immense willpower to leave her breasts so that he could taste the flat planes of her stomach, so that he could circle the delicate indentation of her belly button with his tongue, so that he could breathe in the musky, sexy scent of her womanhood.

He knelt between her legs and took his time, first licking the soft underside of her thighs and then, when her panting was raspy and hoarse, gently inserting his tongue along the crease and then delving deeper to taste her wet, slick sweetness.

Sammy bucked against him. She couldn't keep her hands obediently clasped above her head and instead curled her fingers into his dark hair, driving his mouth deeper against her so that the starbursts of pleasure became sharper and sharper until she was rolling on a tide of pure sensual delight.

She hitched her legs up, intensifying the pleasure, and then cried out when he inserted two fingers into her so that he was caressing her with his mouth and his fingers.

Leo could feel self-control slipping fast. He wanted and *needed* to be inside her.

'I need you *now*.' He barely recognised the shaky tenor of his voice. He reared up and their eyes met. Sammy nodded wordlessly. Even in the midst of searing passion, she noted that he took time out to put on a condom. She was a virgin so perhaps he assumed that she wasn't on the Pill or maybe, even if she *was* for whatever reason, he was a man who never took chances.

He had brought her to the brink and had taken her to a place where nerves at taking him inside her had miraculously vanished. Yes, she still registered that this was going to be a whole new experience for her, but she literally couldn't wait to feel the bigness of him inside her.

He ran a finger along her, delved briefly into her wetness, then nudged her tentatively with the tip of his shaft.

'Leo...' She whispered his name in a voice that was halfway between a gasp and a plea. Her hands were on his shoulders, her body arched up, ripe and ready, as he edged into her, inch by glorious inch.

The feeling was exquisite. Sammy had never actually dwelled on what sex might *feel* like. It had always been a blurry, rosy image wrapped up in the comforting haze of love with a capital *L*. There was nothing blurry or rosy about this. The sensation of his hardness plunging into the very depths of her was mind-blowingly erotic and raw. She pushed against him and that was all Leo needed to ramp up his rhythm. He thrust deeper and harder and felt her whole body quiver around him, their bodies fused.

Sammy was scarcely aware of a brief twinge of discomfort. His need mirrored her own and it was proof of his mastery that he had been able to get her to a point of relaxing enough, trusting enough, to give herself to him without fear of stepping into the unknown.

The feel of her tightness was amazing, as was the heat of her body, the lushness of her feminine curves, the naked desire that had darkened her eyes and caused her nostrils to flare.

He held on, tuned in to her every whimper and cry, knowing just how to drive and angle his big body to intensify the sensations pouring through her as her cries became higher, more uncontrolled.

Her whole body tensed and arched up and only then did he allow himself to let go. The timing was impeccable as their bodies convulsed in unison. It was the most sensual experience Leo could remember having and he wondered whether the fact of her virginity had been a mental turn-on as well as a physical one.

Sagging against him, utterly spent, Sammy

wondered what happened next in this scenario. She hadn't given that a moment's thought. She'd been way too busy rushing into Leo's arms. Now, her nudity embarrassed her and she made tiny movements to distance herself from him and put the sheets between their damp bodies. Leo wasn't having any of it.

'Don't tell me that you're going to go all modest on me,' he murmured, firmly lifting the sheets she had tried to stuff between them and pulling her close against him so that she was in no danger of pretending that what had happened had been a blip she could swipe away. 'I've seen you naked now so trying to cover up is just shutting the stable door after the horse has bolted.' He grinned and lay back flat, tugging her onto him and then draping his arm over her.

Sammy quivered. Her automatic instinct was to analyse what had happened and discuss what would happen next. This was a big deal for her. It was slowly trickling into her that the lines between what was real and what wasn't had become blurred. Where did that leave her? She had handed her virginity to Leo. What did that mean? Was this the beginning to an affair? She'd never considered herself to be *affair material*. Or maybe this was just a one-night stand, something that had happened because they had both been overwhelmed.

She knew that he was not being afflicted by similar internal angst. He wasn't confusing lines or frantically wondering what happened next. When it came to sex, Leo was a man who lived in the moment. He had wanted her, she had wanted him and one and one made two—it was as simple as that.

If she told him that this was a one-off, a mistake, then she knew that he would shrug those broad shoulders of his and put it down to experience. Their charade would continue unimpeded.

And for her…

Would it be so bad for her to snatch a little bit more of this while it lasted? Instead of reacting like Chicken Little with the sky falling down? Leo was offering *fun* and the fact that they were supposedly engaged was an added bonus because it just added verisimilitude to the charade. What was wrong with fun?

She had had a hellish year and a half and now she had a chance to lighten up and enjoy herself for a little while. Where was the crime in that?

His phone buzzed and he rolled to his side and she watched his broad, tanned, muscled back as he read whatever message had been texted to him.

Daringly, she traced a pattern with the tip of one finger. It was probably the least wanton gesture she could have made but she was gratified when he moved and then turned back to her and swung her against him.

'Nice,' Leo growled, turning back to her and catching her finger, sucking it, while keeping his dark eyes firmly fixed on her face. 'I can tell you're destined to be an excellent pupil.'

'What makes you say that?' For someone as forbidding as he was, she was discovering that he could be incredibly engaging.

'You've already picked up rule number four before I've even had a chance to tell you what it is.'

'Have I? What is it?'

Still grinning, Leo primly tucked the sheet under her breasts and circled one of her nipples with his finger. Instantly, it peaked into hot arousal. He moistened his finger and returned it to her nipple and absorbed the little reactions of her exquisite body.

'You're making the first move,' he drawled. 'I like that, but before we have fun—' he settled her against him '—we're going to go downstairs and have something to eat and then we're going to talk about tomorrow.'

'Why?' She flashed him a reckless smile. 'Weren't you the one who mentioned something about no chatting? Wasn't that one of your rules?'

'Like I said, a fast learner. But you're going to have to be the teacher for a while,' he told her wryly. 'The text I just received was from my lawyer. We're going to have Adele solidly for the next four days. A test, it would appear, to judge whether she can adapt to us.'

'Day and night?'

Leo nodded. 'I gather that this is Gail's attempt to throw her granddaughter in at the deep end to prove a point, after which she will repeat her case for having the child stay in Melbourne with her, while she continues to collect even more money from me, no doubt, than she already does, unless she can convince the court that Adele is incompatible with my lifestyle, whether you're on my arm or not, then her case is over and the money will stop.'

'My goodness! And how on earth is it going to be possible to prove anything at all? Is she going to have spies with binoculars peering from behind the bushes and writing reports on what we're doing?'

'A child psychologist will establish how well Adele is likely to cope in the UK and how comfortable she feels around us. So…'

Sammy could see a flicker of anxiety in the depths of his bitter-chocolate eyes although his voice remained neutral.

'So?'

'So I propose we escape to somewhere a little less busy. Head to the coast. I can get my lawyer to source somewhere we can rent. A villa by the sea.'

Without crowds around them and a deadline to meet before Adele was returned to her grandmother, it was going to be much harder for their charade to hold water, especially with a child. Sammy knew, from experience, that most children were a heck of a lot sharper than adults thought when it came to assessing situations and people. Leo wouldn't have to pretend to be in love with her for the sake of lawyers and the public at large. This was going to be a much more difficult task.

'And,' she said slowly, 'you want me to teach you how to relate to Adele? How on earth can I teach you something like that?'

'I didn't come this far to fail at the final hurdle.' He slid out of the bed, prowled naked towards the window, then returned and leaned over her, caging her in, his arms on either side of her body.

'Children aren't like adults,' Sammy told him softly. 'They don't judge and they respond the more natural and open you are with them.'

'Then natural and open is what I will have to be.'

Sammy gazed at him and she thought that it was going to be a lot more complicated for him than merely being natural and open. He would have to relinquish his desire to control everything around him. He would have to go with the flow.

Somehow the thought of that made it easier for her to accept that she wanted him even if it meant stifling her urge to analyse where that *want* would take her. They would both be functioning out of their comfort zone.

She laughed and then sobered up when she saw that he was dead serious. 'Sometimes, it's hard to believe that you and your father share the same genetic pool.'

Leo slipped back into bed. 'I know,' he said drily. 'I guess I'll just have to learn how to operate a little on his emotional level for a while.'

'Is that going to be possible for you?'

Leo didn't answer. The enormity of this undertaking was hitting home—and hitting home hard. To leave Adele in the care of her grand-mother would be a disaster but bringing her back with him was going to require changes to his life he had not considered in depth. Would he be able to cultivate an emotional bond with the child? He'd had a good child-hood, he thought, even though he had hardened over time as he had watched the destructive path his father's emotional excesses had taken him down.

He relaxed.

He might have trained himself to put his emotions on ice when it came to the oppo-site sex—he had seen for himself the catas-trophes that could occur to the hapless bugger who wore his heart on his sleeve—but there was no reason to think that he wouldn't make a perfectly acceptable guardian to Adele and, besides, what he lacked his father would make up for in spades.

'Perfectly possible.' He smiled lazily. 'Es-pecially with you at my side, applying a little discipline whenever you notice me slipping up.' He dropped a kiss on her parted mouth and the kiss deepened until she was throbbing between her legs for him. He pulled back. 'I'll get the ball rolling for somewhere by the sea.' He flicked on his cell phone and began scrolling through his address book. 'And you can get dressed and start thinking of ways of turning me into a good little boy who can pass the next big test.'

CHAPTER NINE

SAMMY LAY BY the pool, her eyes hidden behind the oversized sunglasses she had bought two days previously, shortly before they had col-lected Adele from her grandmother's lawyer.

Everything had to be done by the book.

'One foot out of place,' Leo had said grittily, 'and she'll run screeching to her lawyers that we're flouting the rules.'

In the past couple of days she had heard things about Gail Jamieson that had conclu-sively done away with any lingering doubts about what they were doing. Leo had clearly been loath to part with the information but maybe because they were now more than just partners in a business arrangement he had felt inclined to open up.

Pillow talk.

'Sean was a weak man,' he had told her pen-sively late at night after their first successful day with Adele, the little girl tucked safely in bed hours earlier. 'An only child, spoiled and indulged, with almost no discipline, and I tend to agree with my father that he found himself swept along on a riptide over which he had no control whatsoever. He was completely taken in by Louise and it wasn't hard for him to fall off the bandwagon completely after his mother died. From his communications with my father, it would appear that whilst he knew well enough that neither he nor Louise were equipped to take care of the child they had produced, neither was Gail. There were stories of her leaving the baby unattended while she went out at night and, on one occasion, an actual admission to hospital when Adele was little more than a toddler, after her *falling down some stairs*—although Sean hinted that some corporal punishment had been inflicted by the grandmother.'

'Why on earth didn't he take Adele and leave?'

'Because,' Leo had told her with a wry grimace, 'he was a drug addict. His best intentions were never going to come to anything. Nor could we have undertaken a snatch and grab rescue mission. No, the only way my father felt he could help was to send money over to make Adele's life more comfortable and to sponsor rehabs that never seemed to come to anything.'

'If Gail has been responsible for physical abuse, then surely that would make it easy for you to…'

'Hearsay,' he had told her bluntly. 'To outside eyes, she is the grandmother who rose to the occasion when her daughter couldn't look after her own child.'

Now, looking at Adele in her swimming costume at the side of the pool, Sammy could make sense of the child's personality.

Since they had arrived at the villa, which was an exquisite masterpiece of modernism with spectacular views down to the Surfers Paradise Coast, Adele had barely spoken to Leo at all. She was a cautious, watchful five-year-old, without any of the spontaneity she should have had at her age. There was no running around, no bursts of laughter, no mess made, no noisy intrusions into adult conversations.

Her clothes were neatly worn and never seemed to get dirty. She was the most background child Sammy had ever encountered and her heart went out to her.

And it went out to Leo because she could tell that he was trying hard. Unfortunately, whilst his questions were politely answered, there was minimal eye contact made and absolutely only essential interaction. Now, he was doing lengths, his lean, well toned bronzed body cutting a swathe through the crystal-clear water while Adele stared out into the distance as she clutched the side of the pool.

Sammy could predict the way the rest of the day would go because she was sure that it would follow the pattern of the other days they had had in the villa.

They would enjoy the sun and the swimming pool and then venture down to the town for something to eat and take in another of the local sights. Yesterday had been a stroll on the beach, where they had watched surfers ride the soaring waves. The day before they had paid a visit to the animal park, where Adele had been encouraged to pat a koala, which she had seemed to enjoy. Today they would do something else, some other fun activity, which would end up leaving Leo restless and frustrated because he would, yet again, fail to break through the wall of Adele's politeness.

She smiled as Adele caught her eye and then levered herself up and began walking over. She was wearing a plain black swimsuit and had not removed her bright pink plastic beach shoes, which sloshed as she approached.

'I thought you were going to be a little fishy again—' Sammy grinned '—and show me how you could do those flips underwater.'

Adele smiled and dropped her eyes. 'Leo's in the pool,' she said in a whisper and Sammy reached out and held the child's hands in hers.

'You can't let him be the only fish,' she said with a smile. 'Besides, you make a much prettier fish than Leo. Maybe today we could get you a nice fishy swimsuit. Would you like that? Something nice and colourful? And maybe an inflatable for the pool, as well?'

'Nana might get angry.' Adele chewed her lip anxiously. 'She says it's important not to ask for things. I can only have things if I don't ask for them.'

Sammy's ears pricked up because Adele rarely mentioned her grandmother. 'What if you *do* ask?' she questioned gently. 'Does your grandmother get cross?'

Adele shrugged and remained silent.

'You know,' Sammy said quietly, 'that you have a lovely grandpa over in England who really wants to meet you.'

Adele slid a sideways look at Sammy. 'Nana says that no one wants me but her.'

'Now I *know* that's not true.' She was still smiling, her voice soft and encouraging, but her heart clenched at the behind-the-scenes picture being painted. 'You have a very, very loving grandpa who would burst into tears if he heard you say that.'

Adele's eyes brightened. 'Old people don't cry!' she giggled.

'Just wait till you meet your uncle Leo's dad,' Sammy confided. 'He's a big softie. But maybe you *should* be cautious,' she mused thoughtfully. 'He's famous for hugging a lot. He might just get hold of you and never let you go. You'd be wrapped up in a big bear hug for the rest of your life!'

'How would I eat?' Adele giggled again. It was an unusual sound.

'Your uncle Leo would have to sneak you titbits.'

'How would I go to the bathroom?'

'You'd be allowed to go to the bathroom but you'd have to follow that trail of bread back to his arms.'

'Like Hansel and Gretel.'

'*Just* like Hansel and Gretel.'

'Running away from the bad witch.'

'Who is the bad witch?'

Adele shrugged and her face grew serious, and Sammy knew when to leave things alone.

Later, she repeated the conversation to Leo. It was a little after eight in the evening and Adele was asleep. She never kicked up about going to bed. Indeed, she had to be persuaded on night one to stay up beyond six and as soon as Leo had looked at his watch, at a little after seven, she had jumped to her feet, her teddy clutched to her chest, ready to head upstairs.

She never asked for a bedtime story. She never asked for anything.

'It's almost as though she's too scared of the response she might get.'

'Does that surprise you?' Leo looked at her. The sun had worked magic on her skin, turning her flawless, milky whiteness a toasted golden colour. He couldn't get enough of her. Hours were spent in anticipation of bedding her as soon as they were together. He guiltily wondered whether he was devoting the amount of attention he should have to his little charge when his thoughts always seemed to be wrapped up in images of Sammy and her hot, willing body under his, when his eyes seemed to follow her every small movement. Right now, with the meal finished, he took his time as he watched her over the rim of his wine glass.

She wasn't wearing a bra.

He'd told her that just the thought of being able to reach under her top and feel her glorious breasts was enough to make him harden and she had teasingly threatened to dispense with the bra, a threat he had been extremely keen to take her up on.

'You're looking at me.' Sammy blushed. Her nipples tightened into hard pebbles and she felt that wonderful, familiar dampness between her legs. She had never thought that her body could respond to anyone the way it responded to Leo. His eyes on her made the hairs on the back of her neck stand on end, made her skin prickle as though someone had run a feather over it. The sound of his voice, deep and dark and velvety, could trigger a series of graphic images in her head that made her pulses quicken and her heart beat faster.

She blinked as her sluggish brain began to make all sorts of connections that had been there all along, waiting to be unearthed.

She'd agreed to a phoney relationship and then had agreed to a sexual one because she had been unable to deny her body the thing it seemed to crave.

She'd been swept along on a rosy wave of thinking that she was having fun and not doing anything that any girl her age wouldn't have done. Namely, falling into bed with a hot guy she found irresistible. She was only acting her age!

Had she been especially vulnerable because Leo had been an adolescent crush? Had that added to the thrill? She hadn't stopped to question it.

Of course, it wasn't going to last and that was fine. They were as different as chalk and cheese and if fate hadn't thrown them together then their paths would never have crossed in the way that they had. They would have remained two people who met now and again and exchanged a bit of this and that conversation.

In time, she would have met someone to settle down with. Mr Right. He would have been reliable, kind and with a gentle sense of humour. In keeping with the fact that she had never placed much importance on looks and bearing in mind that she was never going to be asked to sashay down any catwalk, he would have been pleasant enough looking. No gargoyle but no movie star.

So what was she doing falling in love with a billionaire who was out of her reach? A guy who wasn't into commitment, who had thought nothing of throwing money at her to get what he wanted and who had not once mentioned having any feelings for her even though they were sleeping together?

Because fall in love with him she had. Hook, line and sinker, and now the thought of returning to life as she knew it held no appeal, even though she would be getting everything she had dreamed of that money could buy, including the freelance career she craved.

It was a nightmare. What on earth would he think if he could read her thoughts? If he could see into her heart? He was having a fling and she was busy experiencing the greatest love of her life.

'You make me want to stare,' Leo confided roughly.

'Huh?'

'Penny for them.'

'Penny for what?'

'Whatever it is that's going through your head.' He smiled lazily, the smile of the predator sure of its willing prey. 'Is it me?'

Sammy blinked. Her heart was thumping so fast that her ribcage felt threatened. She tried to match his sexy smile with one of her own. It wobbled. 'You're so egotistical.'

'Come and sit next to me.' He patted the space next to him. 'I can't look without touching.'

'Adele's upstairs!'

'And have you ever known a child to sleep as soundly as she does?' Leo asked drily. 'When I looked in on her half an hour ago she was snoring like a trooper.'

Besides, the way the house was designed, it was unlikely that they would be disturbed. It was a clever configuration of all glass at the front, so that every bit of the spectacular view was captured, from the soaring surf of the ocean to the vast blueness of the sky, an uninterrupted panorama because the house was built into the side of a cliff. On the lower floor, everything was open-plan. When one of the immense glass panes was opened, the sea breeze reached every corner of the house. On the veranda, which was railed in with steel, the view was breathtaking.

They were in the snug, which was the only enclosed room on the lower floor and was on a raised, floating mezzanine that afforded them a bird's-eye view of the entire floor but, thanks to one-way glass, no one inside could be seen. A useful office space, Sammy assumed, from which family life could be observed whilst absolute privacy within was maintained.

Not, as Leo had pointed out, there was the slightest chance of Adele surprising them. It was apparent that surprising anyone was something she had been trained never to do.

'We were talking about Adele.' But her voice was tellingly feeble.

'I can't talk with you sitting so far away.'

'Don't be silly.'

'Shall I come and get you? Do you want a demonstration of my caveman capabilities?'

Sammy could think of nothing she wanted more but now her every move was invested with the pain of knowing that all too soon this would be gone. She padded the few feet separating them and sat primly next to him and he pulled her so that she was sprawled against him, lying on top of him but on her back, her body cradled between his powerful thighs.

He slipped his big hands under her tee shirt and she released a sigh of pure pleasure as he massaged her breasts, rolling his fingers over the stiffened peaks of her nipples and rubbing until the wetness between her legs made her want to wriggle.

'We were talking about Adele,' Leo reminded her.

'I... Yes...' Sammy panted. His erection was pressed like a rod of steel against her back, tangible proof of how much he was turned on. 'She... It's a difficult situation for her but, in a strange way, it's, um, actually…I can't think when you're doing that…'

'Playing with your breasts? I'd quite like to take them into my mouth. Think you could flip over so that I can taste them?'

'Leo!'

'You know you want to.'

She did and so much more besides. She flipped over and arched up over him so that her breasts quivered tantalisingly above his mouth and she flung her head back and closed her eyes as he took his time suckling on her nipples, feasting on them, in no great rush. Eyes shut, teeth clenched, she endured the exquisite agony of being teased until she couldn't stand it any more, at which point she settled back down in her original position between his legs, breathing hard and fast.

She wriggled into a comfortable position and her legs dropped open.

'Take off the shorts,' Leo commanded softly into her ear.

Sammy wriggled out of them but when she made to remove the lacy briefs he stayed her hand. Her body was on fire. This was what he did to her. He took away her ability to think and to behave sensibly. He'd done that from the start and he would carry on doing it until he walked away from her. Until they walked away from one another. Except he would continue having an effect on her long after she had disappeared from his life. She couldn't imagine how it would feel to see him the way she had before, in passing glimpses, with Adele.

He pressed his hand flat between her legs, over her knickers, and caressed her until she was moving against his hand, wanting those lazy movements to pick up tempo.

Then he slipped his hand under the lacy cotton. When he inserted his finger and began stroking, she felt like passing out because it felt so good. Her breathing quickened as she savoured the feel of him touching her, the even rhythm as his finger slid up and down, pushing against her core.

He moved and began licking her, revelling in her wetness on his mouth, sliding his tongue into her and feeling the gasp she uttered transmitted directly to his own body, stirring him up. He wouldn't let her come against his mouth like this. But he would fire her almost to the point of no return and then take her.

Their bodies were slick with perspiration when, as she balanced precariously on the cusp of coming against his mouth, he levered h off, pausing only to don contraception w she watched him impatiently, cupping herself between her legs with her hand to alleviate the ache there. Their eyes tangled and he smiled because he knew exactly what she was thinking and what she was feeling.

He nudged at her sensitive opening and then eased himself inside her, his girth filling her up, and when he began to thrust in deep, rhythmic strokes she could only close her eyes and let sensation carry her away.

Their bodies moved as one. Sammy couldn't imagine that sex could ever feel as glorious as this with anyone else, but then how could it when she had given her heart away to him? She came, her body stiffened and then arched up as it splintered into a thousand heavenly pieces and she felt his own orgasm matching her own.

She was as limp as a rag doll as he rolled off her so that they were lying side by side, shoulders and arms lightly touching, both of them staring up at the ceiling. She idly wondered whether the size of the sofa in the room, wider than a single bed, had been fashioned with this sort of activity in mind. Work and play in soundproof silence, invisible to outside eyes. There was something a little naughty about the design of the room and its position inside the house.

She turned onto her side to say something of the sort to him, only to find him staring at her intently, expression speculative.

'What?'

'I expect you're going to be a little shocked at what I'm about to say.'

'What? What are you about to say?' He was so long in answering that her heart had time to gather pace and her nerves had time to start jangling and her brain had time to work out a thousand possible scenarios.

'Will you marry me?'

Sammy's mouth dropped open and she stared at him. She wondered whether her ears had been playing tricks on her but the way he was staring at her, his dark eyes serious with intent, made her pause.

Piercing happiness shot through her. She hadn't dared hope that he might have returned her love! He had been so adamant in his opinions on commitment. He had been so clear-cut when he had laid down the rules of this charade. But if she had been wrong-footed by Cupid, then who was to say that he hadn't been, as well?

'Marry you?'

'I can see that my proposal is shocki~ but—' he slid off the sofa, flexing his r cles, and slung on his trousers, zipping them up but not bothering with the top button and not bothering with his shirt, then he returned and perched on the sofa next to her '—I don't think I considered this whole thing when I embarked on my mission to rescue Adele from her grandmother.'

'What do you mean?'

'My father was desperate to make sure that his granddaughter was brought to England. He'd read between the lines of Sean's infrequent communications to fear the worst and I was inclined to agree with him. The fact that Sean wanted the child to live in England was another argument for the defence, so to speak.'

Sammy was barely following what he was saying. She was too busy wondering where the marriage proposal had been buried. The breathless excitement that had raced through her was giving way to confusion.

'Yes…'

'I expected,' Leo confessed, 'that the difficult part would be getting the grandmother to acquiesce. In other words, I had focused exclusively on winning the custody battle and, with that in the forefront of my mind, all other considerations had taken a back seat.'

'Okay…' It seemed ridiculous that he had

put his trousers back on while she remained on the sofa in her birthday suit, so she, likewise, stuck on her shorts and her tee shirt although she could still smell the tang of sex on her body and could still feel the powerful throb of him inside her.

She sat up straight, hands primly on her knees, and watched him.

'Of course, I did understand that having a child around would alter the dynamics of my life.'

'Did you really?'

Leo grimaced. 'I deserve your sarcasm,' he conceded with a graceful gesture of rueful surrender. 'I was naïve.'

'You're way too accustomed to having everything your own way.'

'I also thought that Adele would be…less stubborn. I have no experience with young children but, in my head, I naturally assumed that this would, indeed, be a rescue mission and the object of the rescue would be overjoyed at being saved.'

'And instead,' Sammy filled in slowly, 'you got a little girl with problems and anxieties. And despite the fact that remaining in this country with her grandmother will probably be the wo thing for her, despite the fact that she prob from the sounds of it, doesn't even *enjoy* living with her, it's still all she's ever known and she's going to cling to the familiarity.'

'I frighten her,' Leo said bluntly. 'The second I try to engage her in conversation, she clams up. The minute I get too close, even if I'm obeying your teacher theory of stooping down to her level, she looks as though she's going to have a panic attack.'

'She just needs to get used to you and she will. Wait and see.'

'Whilst I deeply appreciate your stirring words of encouragement,' Leo said wryly, 'I don't have a great deal of time left over here before the case is decided one way or another. If the outcome is that she is allowed to come back with me, and I very much think that it will be a favourable outcome, then it doesn't give me much time for the bonding process to be solidified.' He looked at her speculatively. 'She likes you. She feels safe with you.'

Sammy didn't say anything. The marriage proposal and that brief flare of thrilling, wonderful joy had withered fast. She knew where he was going and it made her feel faint.

'And so you want to marry me because marrying me would make your life easier with
—le.'

Leo flushed darkly. 'That's not quite how I would have put it.'

'Then how would you have put it?'

'What started as a necessary charade to win this custody battle has stopped being a charade. We're lovers and we both know the sex between us is amazing. On top of that, you have won Adele over. She trusts you and it would certainly make things easier for her if you were to be around when we return to London. Provided, of course, that we return mission accomplished,' he amended dutifully.

'You've paid me a great deal of money,' Sammy said coolly. 'You could just have asked me to stick around for a couple of weeks until she settled in to life over there.'

'I could have,' Leo admitted, 'but it occurred to me that marriage might be no bad thing. I cannot expect to resume my old life as I knew it with a child on the scene.'

'So what you're proposing is a business arrangement.' Sammy's voice had dropped from cool to positively freezing.

'Since when can sex ever be classified as part of a business arrangement?'

Restlessness consumed her and she paced the room, prowling to stand by the glass pane ov looking the living area, distractedly appre

ing the fabulous symmetry of the house while she fought down the hurt and anger of being offered a marriage of convenience.

'I don't suppose it's occurred to you that I might want a little bit more for myself than a marriage of convenience?'

Leo's jaw clenched. He wondered whether he had approached this matter in the right way but how else could he have broached the subject? And why was she now attacking him? He had asked her to marry him. It was a proposal that made sense and not just for him but for her, as well. They got along and the sex was great. She would make a terrific surrogate mother to Adele. Was the prospect of all of that, with unlimited money thrown in for good measure, so appalling?

She was a virgin when she had met him. So obviously the man of her dreams had not sauntered by waving a wedding ring in his hand and patting a cushion in preparation for his bended knee, and surely she was practical enough to wonder whether such a man existed anyway.

Whatever line of reasoning he used, Leo knew that he was aggrieved because he had offered ▪r marriage, the single thing he had never of- ▪ any other woman, and she had turned him down, which no other woman—not one, not a single one—would have done.

'You only want to marry me because it makes sense.' Bitter disappointment made her sound shrill. She hated herself for actually imagining, even for a second, that he had been about to follow up on his marriage proposal with a confession of love. She had truly forgotten the game they'd been playing. She'd truly forgotten that he hadn't jumped into bed with her for any other reason than passing lust and, now that they were lovers, she made sense as a wife because of the relationship she had fostered with his charge.

'Remind me what's wrong with a marriage based on good sense,' Leo gritted. 'Look at my father's disastrous union with Sean's mother and Sean's disastrous union with Adele's mother. The list could go on and on and on. Emotions have a nasty habit of sabotaging good intentions.'

'No.' It would be pointless going into lots of reasons why she wouldn't marry him but for her the biggest one was that he just didn't love her and, when it came to spending the rest of her life with someone, love had to be on the menu.

And he could quote as many disastro

unions as he wanted—that was *his* learning curve, not hers.

He wanted her to be a fixture in his life because he would be inheriting a small child and having Sammy around would enable him to return to his normal life without too much difficulty. She would be there to take the brunt of the childcare away from him. She would be working freelance and could so devote her time to ensuring that Adele settled in as best she could. Leo might have sidelined work a little whilst he was in Melbourne but as soon as his feet hit British soil he would once again immerse himself in his job and if she were around as the dutiful wife he would be unfettered by having to compromise his time.

Marrying her was the lazy, selfish solution to a complex situation he had not given much thought to.

She could understand that he might think that he was conferring a great honour on her because the women he dated would all have probably walked on a bed of burning embers to get to the other side if the ring had been on offer. He wasn't to know that she was in love with him. He wasn't to know that the thought of being with someone who couldn't love her back would have been torture.

Plus, whilst he might be attracted to her now, what was to say that he wouldn't lose interest in a few weeks' time? Without love there to provide the necessary glue to a relationship, would he consider it acceptable to have affairs with women because he had married a woman to basically look after his charge? How could the commitment ever be there between two people locked in a marriage that was an arrangement? When would she start to become a liability? In time, he would form a firm bond with Adele and her usefulness would be at an end. Would he then start regretting his impulsive proposal?

The arrangement he had proposed had more holes than a colander but she still felt sick because she knew that if she turned him down then what remained of their stay in Melbourne would be awkward and stilted and she had become so accustomed to the easy, sexy, flirty rapport they had developed.

But turn him down she would.

'I can never marry you,' she explained quietly. 'I want more from life than being harnessed to someone for all the wrong reasons. If you're worried about how Adele will adjust if you win this fight and get custody of her, then you just need to employ a nanny.' She looke͏ him straight in the eye. 'If you employ a go looking one, you might even find that you want to hop into bed with her. You really don't have to stick a ring on my finger to get what you want. Now, if you'll excuse me, I think I'll go have a shower...and an early night.'

CHAPTER TEN

LEO STARED, SCOWLING, at the computer in front of him. The office was, as was usual late in the evening, quiet. Under normal circumstances, he would have relished the peace and solitude to catch up on the enormous amount of work that required his undivided attention.

Unfortunately, normal circumstances had not been in evidence for some time now.

And yet current circumstances couldn't have been more *normal* in the great scheme of things. He had won custody of Adele. The child psychologist had done a thorough job, had spent time assessing Adele through the child-friendly means of drawing, paper tasks and games. Unbeknown to Leo, it emerged that some testing had previously taken place and had indicated some areas of concern with her grandmother. These areas of concern were not in evidence when it came to Adele's experiences with L and Sammy. The process of bonding had h and the psychologist had been gratified to note that, thanks to her interpretation of the various tasks set, under that quiet five-year-old's exterior was a child who was tentative but keen to face the future with a couple who would allow her to be a child without fear of reprisal. Ironically, the act they had instigated had convinced everyone that the love between them would provide just the security that Adele needed.

Furthermore, the parting of ways between the child and her grandmother had been less nightmarish than expected, thanks to the vast amount of cash he had gifted the woman. Along with assurances that contact would be maintained between her and her granddaughter, with one trip a year being paid for so that they could physically meet. With defeat staring her in the face, Gail had tactfully backtracked from her belligerent stance to become the epitome of helpfulness.

That had been over two months ago.

He had, before even leaving Melbourne, instructed his PA to supervise the redecorating of the room Adele would call her own and, with money thrown at the project, it had been completed in record time.

A week after the agreement had been ‸ed, they had arrived back at his penthouse apartment to a wonderfully child-friendly environment.

Sammy had even gone beyond the call of duty and stayed on the scene for a couple of weeks after they'd returned.

Leo's scowl deepened. She'd thrown his marriage proposal back in his face, politely told him that circumstances had altered and she would no longer feel comfortable being his lover and had then proceeded to act as though nothing had ever happened between them. She had blanked out the amazing sex and turned into a distant friend, acting the part she had been hired to play. She had spent the remainder of their time at the villa keeping Adele occupied, smiling and chatting politely to him and reading her book in the evenings, out on the front deck that gave on to the spectacular ocean views.

He hadn't been able to comprehend why she had turned him down.

What he *did* comprehend, what had become patently clear over time, as she had gradually extricated herself out of his life, was that she had left some kind of ridiculous void.

She was on his mind all the time.

He couldn't focus.

There were many times he wanted to talk

her about Adele, ask her opinion on the child's progress. He knew she'd have been pleased at how *his* progress with Adele had been and he caught himself wishing she was around to congratulate him, with that warm smile that he missed so much.

He had got a top child psychologist on board to come for little 'chats' three times a week, so that he could spot any problems in the making, of which there were, thankfully, none. She would have approved of that. He had taken his time and, with Sammy's help during those first couple of weeks, had employed a young nanny who worked part-time at the school into which Adele had been enrolled. He had made a big effort to try and curtail his working hours and he had spent every weekend with his father, who had been over the moon to have his granddaughter back in England.

Indeed, this was the first late night he had had at the office and only because Adele was in the country staying with his father for a long weekend.

He would be joining them at lunchtime the following day.

It irked him to acknowledge that he couldn't stop wondering whether Sammy had spent the y with Adele and his father. He knew that she was building up her fledgling career as a freelance artist because his father had told him so in passing.

Pride had prevented him from asking for more detailed information.

But pride made a very cold bedfellow and his bed was the coldest it had been since he had reached adulthood. He had no interest in inviting any woman to share it.

With a groan of pure frustration, Leo glanced at his watch to register that it was a little after eight and he had managed to achieve very little on the work front.

This couldn't continue. Accustomed to assuming that for every single problem there was a solution, Leo made his mind up on the spot. It would take him several hours to get down to Devon but the only way he would ever get the wretched woman out of his head was if he actually confronted her.

They had parted company with too many things left unsaid behind the polite smiles and courteous, remote conversation and cornflower-blue eyes that had refused to quite meet his.

He needed to tell her...

Leo's mind braked to a halt and he frowne because he had to dig deep to find the ans to that and digging deep when it came to anything emotional was not in his nature.

So instead he focused on the logistics of getting down to Devon on a Friday evening, debating whether to get his driver to do the honours so that he could try and work in the back of the limo, or else driving himself.

Moving and thinking at the same time, he opted to drive down himself.

He enjoyed driving and being behind the wheel of his high-performance sports car might just clear his head.

There was no need to pack for he kept a wardrobe in his room at his father's house so he didn't have to return to his apartment.

He hit the road and as soon as he cleared the chaos of late-evening London traffic his head also began to clear. Just leaving London behind induced a rush of freedom and he realised that this, at least in part, was down to the fact that he was going to do something about the messy tangle of emotions that had afflicted him ever since Sammy had walked out of his life.

In the morning he would talk to her.

He would pay her a civilised visit. He would ask her how she was doing. Ask to see the studio, maybe talk about her work. Having a civilised conversation with her would fill the nagging hole she had left in his life. It would remove her from the pedestal on which she had somehow managed to get herself placed and he would once again see her for what she was—a nice, uncomplicated and rather ordinary young woman who was ill suited to have any place in his fast-moving, high-octane London life.

She had been a temporary blip and because of the way things had ended, because she had been the one to walk away, he had been left with his nose out of joint.

Wounded pride and a dented ego were curable ailments but he would have to re-establish some sort of normality between them instead of the frozen silence that currently existed.

Frankly, he just felt that he needed to see the woman to get a grip on his wayward emotions.

Adele would be pleased to see him and he found himself smiling. Every shy smile she directed at him was worth its weight in gold.

He had never had much of a paternal streak in him and he had accepted that having the child in his life would be the equivalent of taking on an honourable duty, but Leo was beginning to taste the sweet beginnings of unconditional, uncomplicated love.

He was discovering that there was nothir boring in looking at a three-line story wri in oversized letters that were misspelt. Nor was it a waste of his time fumbling to try to braid her hair and secure the braid with the bright pink ribbons she seemed to like so much. She still didn't talk much but she no longer darted into hiding whenever he appeared. The nanny and the psychologist had worked miracles but the miracle had really started in Melbourne, under the attentive eye of Sammy.

Thoughts flitted through his head as he steadily burned up the distance between London and Devon.

He didn't allow any of them to settle for too long. He knew that at one point he toyed with the crazy notion that the only way he would get her out of his system would be if he slept with her again.

It was beyond incomprehensible because he couldn't conceive of ever chasing behind any woman who had turned him down, especially one who had turned him down when the offer had gone way past the bedroom door and up the aisle in a church.

But the memory of her responsive, hot body still burned a hole through all his attempts at shutting down the temptation to try it on with er again.

He was barely aware of the darkness gathering as he drove fast and smooth past Bristol and into the West Country.

He was also barely aware that he had bypassed the usual route to his father's mansion and was instead following the less travelled road to where Sammy lived with her mother.

He knew the route.

He had taken it on two occasions, the first when they had both arrived down in Devon with Adele and had taken her first to see the grandfather she had never known and then to Sammy's mother. The second time he had managed to find some excuse to take his little charge there. It had been only two weeks previously and Sammy had not been there. He had made a point of not asking where she was.

Leo found himself parked outside the cottage, which was in predictable darkness at a little before midnight, and he honestly couldn't work out at what point his plans for a civilised chat first thing in the morning had changed.

Sammy heard something outside and woke up instantly, although it took her a few seconds to register exactly what it was she was hearing. When she *did* register the source of the noise she was too alarmed and, frankly, confus to do anything but sit up in bed and hold her breath.

Just in case she had imagined the whole thing and she had, in fact, been awakened by a bad dream. One of the many that plagued her largely restless nights since she had returned to Devon.

Her life should have been a bed of roses. Leo had fulfilled all the financial obligations as promised and more. She now had a fabulous studio in which to work, was right there for her mother, whose health was improving hourly because there were no money worries distressing her to bring her down and cause her sleepless nights. She had arranged a part-time teaching job at a nearby school, just so that she could continue having adult company because freelance work could be a solitary career. Two evenings a week, she went into the school and helped with additional lessons for some of the children. The atmosphere at the school was lively, the teachers were young and she loved it there.

But behind the smiles and cheerful façade of the perfect life, she couldn't stop thinking about Leo and the brief relationship they had shared.

She knew that she'd done the right thing in ~rning down his marriage proposal but, where that clear-cut decision should have helped her move on, she seemed caught in a halfway house of muddled emotions and dissatisfied longings. And she also missed Adele. They had formed a bond in the time they had spent together and, although she had seen her a few times since she had returned to pick up the pieces of her life in Devon, she wished that she could see the child more, could play more of a part in her growing life.

The sound of something hitting her window snapped her back to the present and she warily sidled towards the window, making sure not to turn on any lights in the room, and pulled back just enough of the curtain to peer out without being seen.

Her heart began to thump and her mouth went dry because although she hadn't known *what* she had been expecting, it certainly hadn't been Leo.

And definitely not Leo, the epitome of everything that was an alpha male, throwing pebbles at her window. How did he even know *which* window was hers? And then she worked out that it wouldn't have been difficult. The cottage was tiny and only her mother would have occupied, for health and mobility reasons, the bedroom on the ground floor.

She yanked back the curtains and raised the sash window.

'Leo!' For a few seconds her brain seized up. 'What the heck are you doing?'

Good question, Leo thought. He shoved his hands into his pockets and glared up at her, his midnight-black eyes narrowing on her face with the sort of accusation that had Sammy's bewilderment turning to sudden anger.

How dare he show up at her house and throw her into turmoil when turmoil was exactly what she was so desperate to run away from? What gave him the right to mess with her head by just appearing out of nowhere? And why was he here anyway?

At midnight?

When the whole world was asleep?

She flew down the stairs, as silent as a ghost for fear of waking her mother, which was unlikely because she was nothing if not a deep sleeper. Still, it was better to take no chances. When she had returned, mission accomplished, engagement off, she had had the sneaking suspicion that her mother had been disappointed. Although when she had lightly raised the subject, her mumbling concerns had been laughingly waved aside.

But were her mother to wake up and find her

daughter caught in a mysterious tryst with Leo, then who knew what idiotic ideas she might start conceiving?

Which brought her right back to wondering what he was doing on her doorstep, as she pulled open the door and, not seeing him there, carefully stepped out into the night.

Dressed in just her thin oversized tee shirt and with only fluffy bedroom slippers on her feet, the cool early spring air instantly made her shiver. She wrapped her arms around her body and tentatively circled to the side of the house to find him leaning against the wall, so tall, so lean and so ferociously masculine that she felt the breath catch in her throat.

'L-Leo,' she stammered, taken aback by his body language and by the sideways glance he slung in her direction at the sound of her approach. 'What on earth are you doing here?' Her breathing was raspy and uneven, her heart thundered inside her, her eyes were riveted to his lean face, drinking him in the way a starving man might eye up a banquet.

His lack of self-control in ending up here, bringing her outside by a thirteen-year-old's ploy of throwing stones at her window, slammed into him with the force of a sledgehammer and made him stiffen in automatic self-defence.

He had never done anything like this before or ever acted with such a lack of discipline and even now, as his gaze swept over her scantily clad body, he could feel his self-control drop another notch.

'Going to invite me inside?' He pushed himself off the wall but kept his hands firmly in his pockets. 'I decided not to ring the doorbell in case your mother was sleeping.'

'Why are you here?' she breathed shakily.

'I…' He looked away. 'I had to talk to you.'

'At *this* hour?'

'I drove straight down from London,' he said in a non sequitur.

'You could have just called me.'

On the back foot yet again, he bunched his fists and fought down his instinctive urge to try to take command of the situation in any way he could think.

'I needed to see you. I needed to talk to you face-to-face and I thought that if I phoned you, you might be tempted to ignore my call. I wasn't taking any chances.' His glare challenged her to take issue with what he had said but Sammy was so shocked at his raw honesty that she could only stare at him.

She spun round, heart beating fast, and led he way back into the house. She was scarcely conscious of the fact that she was dressed in next to nothing or that the stiffened peaks of her nipples were poking against the soft jersey cotton of her tee shirt.

She'd tried hard to forget the impact he had on her but just seeing him here now, as she shut the kitchen door behind her and leant against it, was reminding her of her aching weakness for him—a weakness she didn't want.

'Surely whatever you have to say could have waited until tomorrow. Is it to do with Adele? I know you've been looking at schools for her in London.'

Don't let your imagination run away with you.

Don't start reading anything behind that intense, disconcerting expression on his face.

'How do you know that?'

'Because your father told me.' Face flaming red, she turned her back on him to put the kettle on for some coffee, hands shaking.

'You've been talking to my father about me?' Leo asked quickly and, he was forced to admit to himself, hopefully.

'No!' Sammy spun round to face him and leaned against the counter by the sink, arms folded, very conscious now of her legs on display. 'He mentioned it in passing. I can't thin' of any reason for you to have just shown up here unless you had some pressing need to ask my advice on schools since I taught in one for quite a while. And that doesn't make sense anyway! That's the sort of thing that could easily have waited until tomorrow. Why won't you just tell me what brought you here?' The atmosphere had shifted and her skin warmed as his eyes roved over her and suddenly she just *knew* why he had come under cover of darkness, *knowing* that he would find her mother fast asleep!

Except surely he wasn't arrogant enough to think that because *she* had been the one to walk away from him that the scales wouldn't be balanced until she warmed his bed again and *he* was the one to walk away? The way he always walked away from women? It seemed incredible but why else would he have descended here at this hour of the night? She truly couldn't think of any other explanation and was frankly appalled when she actually gave houseroom to the tempting idea of taking him up on any advances he might make because she just missed him so much.

'I...' Leo surprised himself by faltering. 'I had to,' he said in a driven undertone and Sammy's brow pleated in consternation. 'You ⁓urned down my marriage proposal.'

'You came all the way here and threw stones at my window to tell me *that*?'

'I told you why I didn't ring the doorbell.'

'But I still don't know why you're here.'

And it's not fair to spring yourself on me because I'm not strong enough to withstand your impact.

'I haven't been able to stop thinking about you.' His fabulous dark eyes held hers. 'I couldn't believe it when you turned me down.'

'Because you're so accustomed to getting your own way,' Sammy said painfully, lowering her eyes and sipping some of the coffee. She noticed that her hands were shaking a little and hoped that he hadn't noticed that, as well. Every nerve and sinew and pore in her body was reacting to his presence, putting her on hyperalert and touching her in places she didn't want. It wasn't fair!

'You can't just show up here and say stuff like that!'

'It's the truth. You make me lose sleep.' He groaned, impatient with the way he suddenly couldn't find the right words to express what he wanted to say. 'When you rejected me I thought that it was something I would be able to shrug off without too much difficulty. I had never let my emotions get in the way of my private life

I had always known where my priorities were. My father had set me a good example when it came to being wary of the pitfalls of acting on impulse and flinging yourself into situations because you were being guided by your heart and not your head. The truth is that I've been thinking about you every day. And every day I managed to convince myself that common sense would reassert itself and I would actually be able to get on with my work and with my life...'

Sammy fought down a wave of disappointment because he was simply confirming what she had already concluded for herself. He had been driven to show up because he hadn't been able to accept the reality of being turned down, especially when it had involved something as serious as a marriage proposal.

'I'm not going to fall into bed with you because...because you miss me,' she said on a hitched breath and Leo flushed. Yes, he missed her. Another weakness of which he was not proud but a weakness, he now realised, he had never had a hope in hell of combating.

He found that he was hesitant to ask her whether *she* missed *him*. What if her answer was *no*? Never before had Leo felt himself treading carefully on such uncertain ground.

Lush lashes shielded his gaze as he lowered his eyes. Sammy itched to reach out to him and she knew that it was just the effect he had on her. He made her want to touch.

'It's not just about missing you.' He recognised what was at the very heart of the restless turmoil that had been undermining his usual single-minded focus for the past few months. 'It's more than that. I feel things for you.'

'You feel *things* for me? What sort of *things*?' Sammy refused to be drawn into feeling hopeful because she had been down that road once and wasn't going to be lured down it again.

'I need you in my life, Sammy.'

'You think you need me because of Adele.'

'This has nothing to do with Adele. My relationship with her is improving by the day. I— no, this is to do with how I feel about you. You came into my life for reasons I could never have predicted and you changed my life and all my priorities. You're warm and funny and smart and all those things should have alerted me to the real reason why I proposed to you.'

'What real reason?' Sammy drew in an expectant breath and held it.

'I love you, Sammy. I fell in love with you out there in Melbourne but I didn't wake up to that because I had always associated falling in love with the kind of excesses I had witnessed, not just in my father and my stepbrother, but in friends, as well.'

'You love me?'

'I love you with all my heart.' His dark eyes were intense with emotion. 'I'd locked away the simple truth that my father adored my mother. I'd sidelined it because the impact of my father's second marriage occurred when I was older and perhaps that's why it was the example I processed more easily. He lost a fortune to that woman who used him ruthlessly and took advantage of his emotional nature. Indeed, he only went into that marriage because he hadn't been able to cope with my mother's death. All in all, I'd resolved from an early age to approach life a lot more phlegmatically than my father had always been prone to do. So when I started loving you it was easy for me to write it off as lust. Lust was something I could deal with. I should have known the minute I proposed to you that I should sit up and take notice.'

'I turned you down because I needed you to love me,' Sammy said, heart full. She reached across the table and they linked fingers. 'I knew that I had fallen for you and I knew that if all you wanted was a suitable mother figure for Adele then it would just be a matter of time before you got fed up having me around and started regretting the fact that you were stuck with me if we married. You don't know how many times I asked myself whether I made the right decision to turn you down.' She grimaced. 'I had to keep reminding myself that you didn't love me and that I would end up getting terribly hurt because you didn't. When you showed up here tonight...' She looked at him with love in her eyes. 'I actually thought that you might have come to try to seduce me. And, if you had, I knew I would have been so tempted to have just caved in.'

'Will you marry me, Sammy? Because I can't live without you. Because you give my life shape and meaning.'

Tears glimmering in her eyes, Sammy smiled and moved round the table to sit on his lap and entwine her hands tightly round his neck. 'I will.'

The following day they announced their engagement—their *real* engagement—to Adele and their parents. They had expected surprise and had anticipated a few seconds of shock. Instead, Sammy's mother exchanged a smug smile with Leo's father.

'I told you,' she said comfortably.

'You win.' Harold chuckled. 'Remind me,' he told his son, beaming, 'never to make a bet with a woman again. This lady never doubted that you'd end up together.'

Adele, sitting pressed between the adults, looked at them for a few seconds and then said tentatively, her little face alive with pleasure, 'When you get married, can I wear pink?'

* * * * *

If you enjoyed this story, why not explore Cathy Williams's other great reads?

SNOWBOUND WITH HIS INNOCENT TEMPTATION
A VIRGIN FOR VASQUEZ
SEDUCED INTO HER BOSS'S SERVICE
THE SURPRISE DE ANGELIS BABY
WEARING THE DE ANGELIS RING

Available now!

LARGER-PRINT BOOKS!
GET 2 FREE LARGER-PRINT NOVELS PLUS
2 FREE GIFTS!

HARLEQUIN

Romance

From the Heart, For the Heart

YES! Please send me 2 FREE LARGER-PRINT Harlequin® Romance novels and my 2 FREE gifts (gifts are worth about $10). After receiving them, if I don't wish to receive any more books, I can return the shipping statement marked "cancel." If I don't cancel, I will receive 4 brand-new novels every month and be billed just $5.09 per book in the U.S. or $5.49 per book in Canada. That's a savings of at least 15% off the cover price! It's quite a bargain! Shipping and handling is just 50¢ per book in the U.S. and 75¢ per book in Canada.* I understand that accepting the 2 free books and gifts places me under no obligation to buy anything. I can always return a shipment and cancel at any time. Even if I never buy another book, the two free books and gifts are mine to keep forever.

119/319 HDN GHWC

Name	(PLEASE PRINT)	
Address		Apt. #
City	State/Prov.	Zip/Postal Code

Signature (if under 18, a parent or guardian must sign)

Mail to the **Reader Service:**
IN U.S.A.: P.O. Box 1867, Buffalo, NY 14240-1867
IN CANADA: P.O. Box 609, Fort Erie, Ontario L2A 5X3
Want to try two free books from another line?
Call 1-800-873-8635 or visit www.ReaderService.com.

* Terms and prices subject to change without notice. Prices do not include applicable taxes. Sales tax applicable in N.Y. Canadian residents will be charged applicable taxes. Offer not valid in Quebec. This offer is limited to one order per household. Not valid for current subscribers to Harlequin Romance Larger-Print books. All orders subject to credit approval. Credit or debit balances in a customer's account(s) may be offset by any other outstanding balance owed by or to the customer. Please allow 4 to 6 weeks for delivery. Offer available while quantities last.

Your Privacy—The Reader Service is committed to protecting your privacy. Our Privacy Policy is available online at www.ReaderService.com or upon request from the Reader Service.

We make a portion of our mailing list available to reputable third parties that offer products we believe may interest you. If you prefer that we not exchange your name with third parties, or if you wish to clarify or modify your communication preferences, please visit us at www.ReaderService.com/consumerschoice or write to us at Reader Service Preference Service, P.O. Box 9062, Buffalo, NY 14240-9062. Include your complete name and address.

HRLP15

LARGER-PRINT BOOKS!
GET 2 FREE LARGER-PRINT NOVELS PLUS
2 FREE GIFTS!

HARLEQUIN
super romance

More Story...More Romance

YES! Please send me 2 FREE LARGER-PRINT Harlequin® Superromance® novels and my 2 FREE gifts (gifts are worth about $10). After receiving them, if I don't wish to receive any more books, I can return the shipping statement marked "cancel." If I don't cancel, I will receive 4 brand-new novels every month and be billed just $5.94 per book in the U.S. or $6.24 per book in Canada. That's a savings of at least 12% off the cover price! It's quite a bargain! Shipping and handling is just 50¢ per book in the U.S. or 75¢ per book in Canada.* I understand that accepting the 2 free books and gifts places me under no obligation to buy anything. I can always return a shipment and cancel at any time. Even if I never buy another book, the two free books and gifts are mine to keep forever.

132/332 HDN GHVC

Name	(PLEASE PRINT)	
Address		Apt. #
City	State/Prov.	Zip/Postal Code

Signature (if under 18, a parent or guardian must sign)

Mail to the **Reader Service**:
IN U.S.A.: P.O. Box 1867, Buffalo, NY 14240-1867
IN CANADA: P.O. Box 609, Fort Erie, Ontario L2A 5X3

Want to try two free books from another line?
Call 1-800-873-8635 today or visit www.ReaderService.com.

* Terms and prices subject to change without notice. Prices do not include applicable taxes. Sales tax applicable in N.Y. Canadian residents will be charged applicable taxes. Offer not valid in Quebec. This offer is limited to one order per household. Not valid for current subscribers to Harlequin Superromance Larger-Print books. All orders subject to credit approval. Credit or debit balances in a customer's account(s) may be offset by any other outstanding balance owed by or to the customer. Please allow 4 to 6 weeks for delivery. Offer available while quantities last.

Your Privacy—The Reader Service is committed to protecting your privacy. Our Privacy Policy is available online at www.ReaderService.com or upon request from the Reader Service.

We make a portion of our mailing list available to reputable third parties that offer products we believe may interest you. If you prefer that we not exchange your name with third parties, or if you wish to clarify or modify your communication preferences, please visit us at www.ReaderService.com/consumerschoice or write to us at Reader Service Preference Service, P.O. Box 9062, Buffalo, NY 14240-9062. Include your complete name and address.

LARGER-PRINT BOOKS!
GET 2 FREE LARGER-PRINT NOVELS PLUS 2 FREE GIFTS!

HARLEQUIN®

INTRIGUE
BREATHTAKING ROMANTIC SUSPENSE

HILP15

WESTERN WP PROMISES

YES! Please send me **The Western Promises Collection** in Larger Print. This collection begins with 3 FREE books and 2 FREE gifts (gifts valued at approx. $14.00 retail) in the first shipment, along with the other first 4 books from the collection! If I do not cancel, I will receive 8 monthly shipments until I have the entire 51-book Western Promises collection. I will receive 2 or 3 FREE books in each shipment and I will pay just $4.99 US/ $5.89 CDN for each of the other four books in each shipment, plus $2.99 for shipping and handling per shipment. *If I decide to keep the entire collection, I'll have paid for only 32 books, because 19 books are FREE! I understand that accepting the 3 free books and gifts places me under no obligation to buy anything. I can always return a shipment and cancel at any time. My free books and gifts are mine to keep no matter what I decide.

272 HCN 3070 472 HCN 3070

Name _____ (PLEASE PRINT) _____

Address _____ Apt. # _____

City _____ State/Prov. _____ Zip/Postal Code _____

Signature (if under 18, a parent or guardian must sign)

Mail to the **Reader Service**:
IN U.S.A.: P.O. Box 1867, Buffalo, NY 14240-1867
IN CANADA: P.O. Box 609, Fort Erie, Ontario L2A 5X3

* Terms and prices subject to change without notice. Prices do not include applicable taxes. Sales tax applicable in N.Y. Canadian residents will be charged applicable taxes. This offer is limited to one order per household. All orders subject to approval. Credit or debit balances in a customer's account(s) may be offset by any other outstanding balance owed by or to the customer. Please allow 4 to 6 weeks for delivery. Offer available while quantities last. Offer not available to Quebec residents.

WPBPA16R